RESCUED

A JT THOMAS NOVEL

E. A. Fleischauer

SECOND EDITION, JULY 2019

Copyright 2019 by E. Alan Fleischauer

ISBN-13: 987-1-7335940-0-4

RESCUED

Chapter One

John Thurgood Thomas looked down from the mountain at the vast expanse of the western plains. He was many days ride from his cabin, taking shelter from a nasty two-day rain in a cave formerly used by a dead miner.

JT, as his friends called him, knew the miner was dead since he had found his body alongside a bed in the cave. Apparently, the man had gathered furniture and belongings left behind by Easterners who had finally realized a four-poster bed and Grandma's armoire were not worth killing their wagon's horses over. As a result, the cave was better-furnished than many of the hotels JT had stayed in. He chuckled as he thought that the miner could have sold furniture instead of mining for gold and made a fortune.

The rain abruptly stopped mid-morning and the sun came out. JT exited the cave, stretched, and checked on his horses. He had owned them since they were born six years ago, and they were in their prime. JT knew they could run until they dropped, and then for a mile more. More than just beautiful horses, they were friends and companions and JT pampered them whenever he could. He knew he would have been dead many times over if they hadn't pulled his iron out of the proverbial fire.

As JT turned back toward the plains, he spotted a lone wagon moving very slowly, hindered by mud and tired horses. What caught his interest were the three women tied to the wagon, with another man walking slowly behind. They were spread out and looked worse for the wear. There was a single driver, two men on horseback, and one man on foot prodding the women to move faster. As he watched, one of the tethered women slipped, fell, and was dragged through the mud.

JT looked through his spyglass, watching the trailing man reach the woman. Instead of helping her, he proceeded to whip her. The others on horseback stopped and, from what JT could see, were laughing.

The wagon driver, now standing, reached for his rifle and pulled the trigger. As the woman started to rise, she was clipped in the shoulder and fell to the ground again.

JT made a decision quickly. He put his .50 caliber Sharps buffalo gun to his shoulder and estimated the drop, distance, and wind in a split second. Aiming above the hombre's head, he pulled the trigger without hesitation and watched impassively as the stranger's head exploded, spraying bone and brain to the wind. As the sound caught up to the bullet, the wagon horses bolted. All hell broke loose as the three women were dragged behind the wagon.

The mounted riders immediately turned to the west and set off for who knows where. The lone man on foot turned in a circle to see where the shot had come from, but JT was hidden from sight.

JT quickly slid another .50 caliber cartridge into the Sharps and did something he was loath to do. Before the wagon horses could take another step, JT aimed a few inches above the closest horse and eased the trigger back. Fire, smoke, and death erupted from the Sharps barrel as JT watched both horses crumple to the ground, shot through the neck. One shot, two sturdy horses down.

With remorse for the horses, JT turned his attention to the lone man on foot who was raising his pistol and striding toward the wounded woman. JT sighed as he slid another cartridge into the Sharps. He quickly made his calculations, aimed above and to the left of the man's shoulders, and pulled the trigger. Once again, fire and death was the result as the man collapsed quicker than the horses had.

He turned his attention back to the two men on horseback. JT knew they were out of range, and from what he could tell from his perch on the mountain cliff they didn't look like they were coming back.

As the women struggled to get up out of the mud, JT noticed a fourth woman who had been sitting on the tailgate of the wagon. She was attempting to grab the lone horse that had not been killed by JT's .50 caliber while trying to pick up the rifle that the wagon driver dropped as he was decapitated.

JT turned to survey his encampment, calculating how long it would take to pack up. He decided he needed to get down as soon as possible and tend to the women, especially the wounded lady. He would go back and fetch his extra rifle and saddlebags when he could, not to mention the unique pistol he had found in the cave.

JT put down his Sharps and grabbed his Winchester, then turned toward the wagon and fired three shots into the air. At the top of his voice, he yelled, "I'm coming!" As his voice echoed off the mountainside, he had no idea if the women could hear him.

He saddled up his horses and crept around the narrow ledge that curved around the mountain cliff, taking his time and peering over the steep drop-off. JT kept an eye on the horses' footing until he hit the ground, where the cliffs ended and the plain started.

Then his thoughts turned to the four women. They obviously had been held captive against their will, but beyond that, it was anybody's guess how they ended up with four desperadoes. Were they sisters and mothers abducted from a wagon train? Were they prostitutes or schoolmarms? *I guess I'll find out in time,* JT thought.

Losing patience at the bottom of the cliff, JT kicked his horses into a long and yard-eating gallop. He sensed that the horses had picked up on the urgency of the situation and were giving him their all.

He pulled up a hundred yards from the wagon and fired a shot into the air. "I'm a friend and I'm here to help," he shouted.

"OK, but we are armed, so put away that rifle," shouted the woman who had been sitting on the tailgate.

JT slid the Winchester back into the scabbard and deftly slipped the hammer strap off his Colt, not knowing what he was riding into. As he approached the wagon, he saw that the women in the mud were exhausted and emaciated, two of them not even getting up from the ground.

The other woman walked toward him, holding her confiscated rifle. "Who are you?" she asked.

"Well, I'm the guy that saved your butt and I mean you no harm. My name is JT Thomas, and from the looks of you I got here just in time."

"My name is Jean Cantrell," said the woman, "and yes, you did. These women were on their last legs and I think those men were going to kill some of us sooner rather than later."

JT looked in the direction the men had ridden off to, checking whether they had regrouped. "Yeah, I think you may be right," he said, swinging down from the saddle. "I know you are glad to be rid of them but we need to get all of you out of here in case they come back. Also, this is Indian country and I'd be surprised if those shots didn't attract them."

"I agree, but Dawn is hurt," Jean replied.

JT turned back to Pete, his packhorse. He slid his medical bag and a bottle of whiskey out of the saddlebag. "Let me take a look at her. I was in the war and I saw a lot of gunshot wounds," he said.

As he approached, Jean pointed to the wounded woman. "JT," she said, "this is Dawn. That's Emily next to her."

Both women nodded and JT squatted down next to Dawn. "Nice to meet you, Dawn," he said. "I'm going need to cut your sleeve to get at that wound. That OK with you?"

She nodded. "Please do. What's the whiskey for?"

"To sterilize the wound," JT replied.

"Boy, that's a waste of good whiskey. How about if I take a snort or two first?" Dawn asked.

"Be my guest," said JT.

As Dawn downed the amber liquor, JT cut open her sleeve. "This doesn't look too bad," he remarked as he cleaned it. He poured a hefty dose over the gunshot wound and bandaged it tightly. "That will do for now. I'll leave the bag and whiskey here with you."

He turned to the rest of the women and motioned toward Pete. "Let's hook my packhorse and that other horse to the wagon and get out of here."

After using Pete to drag the dead horses away from the wagon, they made quick work of putting the horses into their harnesses. The horses sensed their urgency and pawed at the muddy ground, anxious to get moving.

JT quickly tied his other horse to the wagon. With Jean's help, he lifted Dawn into the back of the wagon, then helped the other two women up. Jean climbed into the driver's seat, called out to the horses, and with a shake on the reins they were off.

JT jumped into his saddle and quickly rode close to the wagon. Jean nodded over her shoulder at the last woman and said, "This is Annabelle."

JT saw a striking woman with stunning red hair cascading down her back. She was a bit muddy but nonetheless beautiful. "Hello, Annabelle," he said, smiling.

Annabelle looked up while tending to Dawn. "Nice to meet you," she said while frowning at Jean. "You did a nice job with the bandage." She picked up JT's medical bag and inspected the contents.

As the horses picked up the pace, Jean said "Annabelle knows what she's talking about. She is a healer. Spent three years with the Cheyenne when she was a teenager and learned quite a bit about their medicines and potions."

"Where are we headed?" Annabelle called out over the noise of the fast-moving wagon.

JT had thought about taking the woman back to the cave, but he knew Dawn's wound needed real medical attention. He said, "We'll head to the nearest town with a doctor, Point Stevens Pass. With this wagon slowing us down a bit it should take a day and a half. We will stop well before dark. I know a nice spot."

As they rode on, JT thought, *What have I gotten into? What the hell is this all about anyway?* Everyone but Jean seemed to be exhausted and emaciated. No one was speaking and it seemed like everyone was lost in thought.

A few hours later, with a brief stop to water the horses, JT pointed to a copse of trees about a quarter mile off the main trail. It was surrounded by scattered boulders and sat at the bend of a small creek that was usually teeming with trout.

A faint trail led to the creek, and as JT pulled up the horses Jean spotted a circle of rocks that had held more than one campfire. "Have you been here before?" Jean asked as she helped Annabelle move Dawn out of the wagon and onto a small flat boulder near the fire pit.

"I have, JT said. "Why don't you get Dawn settled in and get a small fire started? After I take care of the horses I'll see if I can't catch a trout or four."

While Annabelle tended to Dawn, Jean gathered firewood and Emily got the cookware out of the wagon. The fire was lit and soon ham and beans were set to boil. JT soon returned from the creek with a couple of nice-sized trout, cleaned and ready for the pan.

"That was fast," exclaimed Emily.

"Yeah, they are hungry fish," JT commented as he tossed the trout into a skillet and set it on the fire.

As they sizzled, Emily exclaimed, "Oh my God, that smells wonderful!" Annabelle and Dawn agreed wholeheartedly.

Jean tapped her knee with her new rifle. "Food will be done shortly. Why don't you all shut up and thank our rescuer?"

The women nodded and murmured, "Thank you, JT."

"You're welcome," JT replied as he lifted the trout off the flames. "Dinner is ready!"

Everyone ate their fill and coffee was made. Annabelle exclaimed, "What a wonderful meal. They hadn't fed us any solid food for days!" as Jean frowned.

"Glad you liked it," commented JT, wondering what that frown was about. He put that thought aside and got the whiskey, offering it to the women. All but Annabelle nodded, and JT added a splash to each coffee cup.

"So, how did you end up with those desperadoes?" JT asked.

Jean quickly spoke up. "It's a long story and it's getting late. Let's get some sleep and we can talk about it tomorrow." She tapped her knee with the rifle again.

JT frowned as Annabelle looked away. "OK, that's fine," he replied as he sprinkled creek sand on the fire, leaving enough embers to keep the coffee warm throughout the night.

"We need to take shifts on watch," JT said. "I'll take the first and third. Jean and Annabelle can take the second. Emily, I'd like you to drive the wagon tomorrow so I can scout ahead on Pete. You need to get some sleep. Annabelle can tend to Dawn in the wagon. Jean, you can ride shotgun since you seem to be familiar with a rifle," he said snidely.

The night went by uneventfully with even the injured Dawn sleeping through the night. The women awoke to the smell of coffee being prepared by the early-rising JT.

9

"I'm making pan bread and bacon this morning," he said. "No eggs, but plenty of coffee. I'd like to get started sooner rather than later, so let's move it along. The farther we get from the men that captured you the better I'll feel."

After quickly eating every morsel, the ragtag group cleaned and packed. JT saddled the horses, and the group soon returned to the main trail for a long day in the sun.

As the morning wore on, JT rode up to the side of the wagon and said to Jean, "So now, tell me about how you ended up with those men."

Jean looked straight ahead and did not answer.

"Well?" JT inquired.

Jean turned a cold eye toward JT. "I don't want to talk about it," she said.

Frowning, he glanced over his shoulder at Annabelle, who was tending to Dawn in the rear of the wagon. She simply shrugged her shoulders with a frown on her face. *Well, well,* thought JT. *Doesn't that beat all?*

As Annabelle snorted derisively in the back of the wagon, JT turned Pete toward Point Stevens Pass. He looked over his shoulder at the wagon, and no one was saying a word.

Riding out ahead to scout, he looked up at the sky. The afternoon sun was a disk of relentless heat that surrounded the four women. JT was simply perplexed.

Chapter Two

Point Stevens Pass was a small town in the Colorado high plains. Lewis Stevens established it when he gave up on crossing the mountain on his way to California in search of gold, fame, and fortune.

When a wheel on his wagon gave out, he hiked a mile to the pass, pitched a tent, and didn't move for over twelve years. He sold his wagon, broken wheel and all, to more adventurous souls in exchange for a few ornery mules. From there, he backtracked to the sprawling town of Columbus, Colorado, over 100 miles away. He charmed the local merchants into loading him up with goods and food on credit, then returned to Point Stevens Pass and proceeded to gouge anyone who would pay his inflated prices. Many travelers used the pass on their way west, so there was no lack of takers, or suckers, as Stevens was known to call them once they rode out.

JT had been to Point Stevens Pass once or twice and had met Stevens a few times. He had, in fact, bought him a drink. JT considered Stevens an acquaintance, just not a friend. The feeling was mutual, he suspected.

With the sun at its zenith, they reached town. JT circled back to the wagon, took his Winchester out of the scabbard and rode just ahead.

"This is a friendly town for the most part, unless it's not," he yelled over his shoulder to the women behind him. "But there aren't more than a dozen women here, so keep your heads down and listen to me." *A fat chance of that,* he thought as they made their way down Main Street.

The small caravan passed a tonsorial shop, a small tailor shop, and a boarding house that displayed a chalkboard that read "Vacancies." Underneath, there was a neatly-painted wooden sign that said "Clean But Not Cheap." JT smiled to himself. The slow-moving caravan passed a café that had another nicely painted sign that said "Eatery."

JT nodded to himself. *They take good care of their establishments,* he thought. The townsfolk had noticed the caravan and began to drift out of the shops onto the boardwalk. JT nodded to a few who looked reputable. He didn't nod to the others that came out of the Stevens Saloon. The place had a brand new well-painted sign that depicted a naked woman, anatomically correct, holding a spear. JT thought for a moment and realized it was a point. *Point Stevens Pass,* he surmised.

Past the saloon was Stevens Bank, and across the street was a mercantile and a pharmacy. Farther down was a jail that looked brand new, and next to that was a place with a sign that read "Doctor, Dentist and Veterinarian."

JT turned to the women, who had remained remarkably silent. "I'm stopping at the livery and then the jail," he said as they pulled up to the doctor's office. "You all get Dawn in there and I'll meet you at the boarding house."

JT helped Dawn down and the group of women walked stiffly into the doctor's. JT climbed up on the wagon after tying the horses to the back. With a shake on the reins he turned toward the livery stable.

The place was nicely painted and orderly. JT also noticed it wasn't called Stevens Livery. Rather, a neat sign read "Buck's Livery." JT pulled up the caravan consisting of the wagons, both of his horses and the third horse. An immense, broad-shouldered, completely bald man greeted him at the door. He was over six foot six and 350 pounds or more, JT estimated.

"Hello, I'm Buck," said the man forcefully. "Now, that's a lot of horses for one man."

JT nodded. "Yeah, it would be, but I didn't come alone."

"Well, I've got room for 'em all," Buck said.

"Good, give them all your best care, grain along with hay. And if you can scrounge up an apple or two for Pete and Pete here, I'd appreciate it," JT said, nodding at his horses.

"Sure thing, but did you just call them Pete and Pete?" Buck inquired.

JT chuckled. "Yeah, they are twins, unexpected twins. They are actually Pete and Re-Pete, but sometimes I can't remember which is which."

"Well, they are mighty fine horseflesh, and I'll take good care of them," said Buck, pocketing the $20 gold piece that JT had flipped him before climbing down from the wagon.

"We'll be here for at least a few days, if not more. I'll check on them in the morning," JT said as he strode toward the jail.

"Sheriff Cole is out at Stevens Ranch," Buck hollered after him. "Probably won't be back 'til tomorrow afternoon."

"He likes the good whiskey that they serve," Buck mumbled to himself.

JT turned and saw Annabelle, Emily, and Jean leaving the doctor's office and heading toward the boarding house. He caught up with them just as they got to the neat, well-cared-for house. "What happened to Dawn?" he inquired.

Jean stepped forward quickly. "The wound was worse than it looked, and the doc gave her quite a bit of laudanum to fight the pain. She went out like a light; won't wake up for hours," she said with a smirk.

"OK," JT replied, noticing the smirk. "I hope she is all right. Let's see if they can accommodate us at this boarding house."

The bedraggled group made their way to the quaint house, where they were greeted at the door by an attractive woman in her early forties.

"Good afternoon," the woman said, smiling. "I'm Emma and this is my boarding house and my home."

"Well, well!" JT exclaimed. "I'm JT, this is Jean, this is Annabelle, and this is Emily. They have all been through quite an ordeal and need a roof over their heads, a meal in their stomachs, some new clothes, and a good night's sleep, not necessarily in that order. We also have Dawn with us, but she was shot and is with the doctor."

"Oh, my!" exclaimed Emma. "I hope she is OK! Anyway, I have rooms for all of you." She moved behind the reception desk. "How many rooms would you like?"

Annabelle moved toward JT. "We don't have any money," she whispered in his ear.

"Not to worry, it's on me," JT quietly responded, then turned toward Emma. "I'll take a room for me and I guess two for the women."

Jean moved toward the reception desk. "Do you have a room that will sleep all four of us women?" she asked.

"Oh yes, indeed I do," replied Emma. I have a large room with two twin beds and a four-poster. Will that do?"

"Yes," Jean indicated. "That would be fine and will save JT some money."

"The rooms are normally four dollars a night, which includes dinner and breakfast. You seem like nice folks, so I'll only charge you two dollars per room. The sign is to keep the riffraff out," Emma said with a smile.

JT paid for three days and they made their way down the hall to their rooms. Jean paused while letting Annabelle and Emily into the room first. Blocking the door, she turned toward JT.

"You can see they are exhausted, so we will see you at dinner. I may run out to get some clothes for all of us while they nap," Jean snapped. "Can you loan us a few more dollars for the clothes?"

"Sure. Here is $10, that should be more than enough," he said and made his way up the stairs to his room, thinking, *Easy come, easy go.*

Jean closed the door, set her rifle down next to the door and removed the Colt .45 from behind her back, pointing it at the frightened women in the room.

"All right, you two. If you behave, I'm not going to kill you. You've been good so far but I'm not sure when Dawn is going to wake up and spill the beans to the good doctor. So be good for a little while more and I will be out of your hair forever. Now take off your pants, shirts, shoes, and socks and lie down on the beds."

The frightened women quickly complied and Jean stuck their soiled socks in their mouths. "I hate to do this, but…," she blurted out as she hit both of the helpless women solidly on the back of their heads, knocking them out. She then tied them up with the shirts and pants as well as she could.

She strode to the door and quickly glanced out. Seeing that no one was in the narrow hallway, she locked the door from the inside and pulled it shut firmly behind her. She made her way to the small lobby, stopping when Emily looked up from some paperwork on her small desk.

"Hello," Emma said with a perplexed look on her face.

"Hello," Jean curtly replied. "Annabelle and Emily are mighty tired. I'm going to check on Dawn and perhaps get us all a simple change of clothes."

Emma stood. "Well, that makes sense. The clothing shop is on the other side of the street. You can see it from the porch, and you know where the doctor's office is."

"I'll be back in time for dinner. Please don't disturb the ladies; they were sleeping when I left," Jean said vehemently.

"Oh, of course not!" exclaimed Emma. "They did look exhausted and naps are wonderful. But they sure look like they need to eat, so please hurry back."

Annabelle woke on the bed, and it took her a moment to remember why she was gagged and bound. She turned her head and looked at Emily, who looked to be unconscious but was still breathing. She yelled through the gag, but it muffled her screams and caused her tender head to throb terribly, so she stopped. She knew someone would find them; she simply needed to be patient.

She reflected on the past few days, wishing to God she had never stopped her wagon when the gang on the trail approached her. She had recognized Dawn on one of the horses and it caused her not to reach for her rifle.

Annabelle was a healer to the Indians, a nurse as needed to the town residents, and a midwife to the women on the local farms and ranches. She had traveled with her protégé Emily to deliver a healthy, bouncing baby boy at a small ranch on the outskirts of the town of Colby.

The pair was often seen on the trails and roads outside of town, since farmers and ranchers seemed to breed like rabbits, with a goal of eight, nine, or even ten children. Sons were coveted and daughters and wives were tolerated, but everyone worked from sunup to sundown as soon as they were old enough. *Cheap labor,* Annabelle thought.

The men tolerated Annabelle and Emily because nurses and doctors were few and far between. Besides, they were very good at what they did.

Emily worshiped the ground Annabelle walked on, and Annabelle was all too happy to have her help. She made good company, knew when to stop talking, and anticipated Annabelle's every move. In essence, she was a godsend. But Annabelle truly wished she hadn't been along on this trip.

The gang approached Annabelle on the trail, and it was obvious they were in a hurry and in trouble. Two of the men looked injured and their horses had been peppered with a lot of buckshot. They moved up quickly, and before she had a chance to react they surrounded the wagon, guns raised.

The apparent leader moved up to the wagon and leaned into Annabelle's space. "Well, what do we have here?" he exclaimed, eyeing Annabelle's red hair and womanly figure.

Annabelle ignored him and turned to Dawn, who was seated in front of a scarecrow-skinny man with long dirty hair. "What's going on here, Dawn?" she asked.

Dawn exclaimed, "They killed the sheriff and the deputy! They robbed the bank and killed my fiancé Robbie!"

"Enough of that," interrupted the leader. "We're taking your wagon, so get off. We've got two men shot up and we're in a hurry."

"Well, I'm a nurse and so is she," Annabelle said, nodding at Emily. "Perhaps we can help."

"Why, that's the best news I've heard today. Get those men into the wagon. You too," he said, pointing to Dawn.

He turned to Annabelle. "Well, I guess we don't need to shoot you … yet. You take care of them and maybe we'll let you live. What do you think, sis?" he said to the lone woman of the gang, who frowned, then nodded grimly.

"By the way, I'm Cain Cantrell, and I lead this bunch," the man said proudly. "Now let's get out of here," he yelled.

After the two wounded men were loaded into the wagon, Annabelle and Dawn got in and Emily grabbed the reins. She turned the wagon around in short order and moved out at a fast clip.

Annabelle looked over her shoulder. She saw that the woman had stayed behind, stowing her rifle and pulling a Colt from behind her back. As she watched, the woman put the muzzle to the shot-up horse's head and sent it to horse heaven. The dead animal almost knocked down her mount as it fell, but the woman calmly righted it. She then leaned down and put two shots into the dead horse's side.

Annabelle cringed as she watched the woman lean across her skittish horse and put shots into the flank of the other wounded horse. It stayed on its feet and bolted, but the woman calmly took aim and put two more shots into its backside. Turning to look at Annabelle, she smiled wickedly and blew smoke off the front of her Colt. Annabelle shivered and thought to herself, *This woman is evil.*

Annabelle turned her attention back to the wounded men in the wagon. One was hurt badly; he had taken a bullet to the chest, just below his right shoulder.

Annabelle was amazed that he hadn't died immediately, but apparently he had ridden a horse for miles. *He must be one tough hombre*, she thought. The other gang member had taken a face full of buckshot. Annabelle looked at the young man, who was covering his face and wailing. "You're going to be OK," she stated. Turning to the older man, she thought, *You, I'm not so sure about.*

JT appreciatively noted the water pitcher, large ceramic bowl, and towel on top of the chest of drawers in his boarding house room. He washed up, then sat on the bed and took off his boots and socks while glancing out the window toward Main Street.

Jean was coming out of the mercantile, dressed in black denims, riding boots, and a green long-sleeved man's shirt. She held a black Stetson with a band of coins around it. She didn't head back to the boarding house or the doctor's office, but crossed the street and disappeared from JT's view. *Where in the heck is she going?* he wondered.

He was surprised to see the door to the doctor's office open into the bright sunlight. JT stood to his full six-foot one height as he watched the bespectacled, elderly man he assumed was the doctor. He had an arm around an agitated, ashen Dawn and was moving slowly toward the boarding house. All thoughts of a quick nap before dinner gone from his mind, JT quickly put his socks and boots on. He buckled on the Colt, picked up his rifle, put on his hat, and hurried down the stairs.

Chapter Three

Jean noticed the bank was empty except for the teller. *Closing time,* she surmised. She strode briskly to the teller's cage.

"Hello," she said to the attractive young woman. "I'd like to make a substantial deposit and I'd like to speak with the person in charge."

"That would be Mr. Gleason. I'm Millie, his daughter," the teller responded. "He's in his office. Please wait here."

As Millie headed toward a large room in the rear of the bank, Jean spun on her heels. She locked the door and flipped the "Closed" sign, hiding it with the curtains.

Millie returned. "Mr. Gleason will see you now," she said, then turned and led the way. As she knocked on the thick oak door a voice said, "Come in." She opened the door and moved inside. "We have a potential customer who would like to make a substantial deposit!" she announced proudly.

Jean entered the office and quickly removed the Colt from behind her back with practiced ease. She smiled as she closed the office door and locked it behind her. "Well actually, I'd like to make a substantial withdrawal," she stated with a smirk.

"Oh my," declared Millie. "Oh my," Mr. Gleason echoed.

"Yes indeed, oh my" agreed Jean. "I'm in a bit of a hurry so here is what you will do. Open that safe and do it quickly," she demanded, putting the muzzle of the Colt to Millie's head. "NOW!"

With hands shaking and sweat forming on his forehead, Mr. Gleason spun the dials. He moaned as he fumbled the combination and the telltale click wasn't heard. "Oh my, oh my!" he exclaimed.

"Do it again, and get it right or you're going to your daughter's funeral," Jean stated vehemently.

He tried again and this time the tumblers fell into place. "Thank God!" he cried out. Then he suddenly collapsed to the floor.

"What the hell?" Jean exclaimed.

"He has a bad heart," Millie blurted out as she watched her father turn gray and pale. "He needs a doctor!" she cried, looking up at Jean.

Jean, however, was too busy staring at the contents of the safe to notice. The vault was loaded with row upon row of gleaming, neatly stacked gold bars. She stood stock-still for a minute, at a loss for words. Then it dawned on her that she had no way of getting all that gold out of the bank. Quickly grabbing one of the banker's bags, she turned it inside out to hide the bank logo. Then she quickly hoisted two of the heavy bars into the bag along with the meager amount of cash that had been stacked.

"Where's the rest of the cash?" Jean demanded.

"At the teller stations," Millie replied. "We were just closing."

Jean stood silent for a minute before saying, "The hell with it." Leaning over the unconscious banker, she removed his belt, one boot, and a sock. She ordered Millie to turn around, then tied her up with her father's belt, stuffing the sock into her mouth.

"I'm not planning on killing you, but I'll be out in the hall, and if I hear you move I'll come back and finish you. I mean it," Jean growled. "Though I'd hate to have to; you're too beautiful to kill. We could have had quite a good time together," said Jean lasciviously. "If I had more time, I'd take you with me."

Jean moved to the office door and opened it up a crack. Seeing that the bank was still empty, she crossed to the lobby and headed for the door. To her surprise, she found herself looking directly at a tardy bank customer who was peering through the window. He was holding up a small bank bag, waving and pointing toward the door.

"Oh crap," Jean uttered. Retreating toward the back of the bank, she spotted a rear exit. "Alleluia," she whispered, taking time to peek back in the office.

No one had moved and Mr. Gleason looked like he was going to be attending his own funeral. Jean locked the office door from the inside and slammed it shut.

Within seconds she was out the back door with the bank bag and its precious contents. She headed briskly for the livery stable, trying not to attract attention, deciding how she would deal with the liveryman. She smiled. "Men are so easy," she said to herself, undoing the buttons covering her cleavage. "So easy."

JT hurried down the stairs to the front desk, where Dawn and the doctor were ringing the desk bell quite loudly. He touched Dawn on the back of her shoulder, then reached around and put his other hand over the bell. As Dawn turned around, she threw herself at JT, hugging him tightly and sobbing uncontrollably. JT returned the hug and looked over Dawn's shoulder at the doctor.

"Hello," JT said. "I'm guessing you're the doctor?"

"Yes, Doctor Spencer DeWitt at your service," the man stated formally while holding himself to his full five-foot-one height. "More importantly, I am at this wonderful woman's service."

JT gently pushed the sobbing Dawn away from his chest, offering her his kerchief. "Now pull yourself together and tell me all about it," he said with a kind smile.

Over Dawn's shoulder, JT saw Emma hurry up the front steps from the garden. She leaned on the desk and struggled to catch her breath. "What's...going...on?" she asked.

Dawn moved toward Emma. "Jean robbed the bank!" she blurted out between receding sobs.

"What are you talking about? Our bank?" Emma asked.

"No, MY bank," Dawn responded. "In Colby, where I'm from. I was born there, my fiancé lives there, my parents live there; I work there! Colby, Colorado," she repeated, almost hysterically.

JT stepped forward. "Slow down," he insisted. "Just take your time. OK, you're from Colby, that's good. I've been there, it's a nice little town. But slow down and tell me more."

"Yes, tell us more," DeWitt chimed in, gazing into Dawn's baby blue eyes. He was obviously smitten with his new patient.

"Please do," added Emma, so quietly Dawn needed to lean forward to hear her.

Taking a deep breath and clutching JT's hankie as if it gave her support, Dawn continued. "They came into our bank, right at closing time. It was a payday, end of the month and we had been very busy. We would have been closed but there were customers still in the bank and we were busy getting them taken care of. I didn't even get lunch, and I had made a wonderful chicken sandwich for lunch. I like to cook and I had made my fiancé dinner the night before, he loves barbecued chicken. So…."

"Whoa, stop there," JT cut in. "Just take your time, Dawn, and tell us about the bank. I'm sure you are a fabulous cook, and I'd love to try your cooking and meet your fiancé some time, but tell us about the bank first…OK?"

"Oh my God!" Dawn exclaimed, and proceeded to break down again, sobbing and wailing, bending over and clutching her stomach. "They killed him!" she screamed. "Robbie, my fiancé, they killed him."

No one moved. Everyone stood spellbound, frozen to their spot on the floor. Then DeWitt ushered Dawn over to the settee in the lobby. "Relax," he said soothingly. "We are here. We are friends, and no one will hurt you," he said with calm conviction, wiping a tear from his eye. He turned toward JT. "Tell her she is OK," he said. "Tell her she is safe."

JT knelt down and held Dawn's hand. "You are safe, Dawn, no one will hurt you, I promise." He turned to DeWitt. "Can you give her something?" he asked.

"Yes, absolutely. Let's get her back to my office."

JT turned to Emma. "Can you help him, please? I need to check on Emily and Annabelle."

"Let me give you the keys," she responded.

As DeWitt slowly moved Dawn off the settee, Emma reached behind the reception desk and took the spare key out of its slot. "Do you need my help?" she asked.

"Actually, I do. I'm not sure what we are going to find in their room," he replied hesitantly. "Doctor, will you take care of Dawn?"

"Of course," DeWitt exclaimed as he helped Dawn down the front stairs. "Make sure they are OK! You know where to find me."

Jean strode into the livery and was met by a smiling Buck. "Well hello, little lady," he exclaimed, looking down at Jean's chest, not into her eyes at all.

"Hello," Jean replied demurely. "My name is Jean Cantrell. I came in with the other women and the big handsome man called JT."

"Oh yes, I met him," replied Buck. "Seemed like a nice fellow. But handsome? Now, *I'm* handsome," he chuckled.

"Oh, yes you are. But right now, I need that horse saddled," she said, pointing to the mount she had ridden in. "Could you do that for me?"

"Ah, sure," Buck replied. "Are you sure it's OK with JT?"

"Well, it is my horse, after all. But of course he is OK with it, he sent me over. He will be here in a minute or two and will want his horses saddled too."

"All right then, give me a minute, I'll have him saddled and ready to go." He made quick work of saddling the sturdy horse and offered to hoist Jean up into the saddle.

"No, I can do it, but thank you," she said, smiling. She kissed Buck on the cheek, making him blush. "You are a handsome devil," she murmured.

As she swung up into the saddle, she pointed to the bank bag and asked, "Can you hand me that?"

"Why sure, but don't you want me to put that stuff in your saddle bag?" he inquired. "Sure looks heavy."

"No time, but thanks. When JT shows up, give him a message for me, OK?"

"Sure, no problem."

"Tell him thanks for nothing."

Then she galloped out of the stable and was gone, heading back toward the trail she had come in on.

Chapter Four

Keys in hand, JT knocked on the women's door, quietly at first and then more loudly. Pressing his ear against the door, he heard muffled voices.

"Hello!" he yelled out at the top of his powerful voice. "Can you hear me?" He knelt down and listened again and the muffled voices seemed louder. He motioned Emma away from the door, drew his Colt, then backed up a step and kicked the door open. He rolled into the room, hoping to avoid a bullet to the chest.

As he stood up, he saw that only the two women occupied the room. They were lying on their stomachs on the beds, tied up with their pants and screaming as loud as they could through the socks stuffed into their mouths. He was shocked to see they were naked as jaybirds.

Emma moved to his side. "JT, why don't you turn around, step outside, and watch for Jean? I will take care of this."

JT stepped into the hallway, gently closed the door, and thought about the situation. Dawn's revelation about Jean made a lot of things fall into place. All this time, she had seemed to be the only outlier in the scenario. She just didn't fit with the other women. They were clearly famished but Jean seemed to be well fed. She acted like she was in charge and carried the rifle at all times. She always wanted the group to stay together, curtailed any interaction between JT and the others, and refused to talk about what happened on the trail.

He started thinking about how he had gotten into this mess. One minute he was on what Australians would call a walkabout. *I guess it was actually a rideabout,* he chuckled to himself. The next thing he knew he was rescuing four women from desperadoes.

He thought back to the cave. He had nearly missed it in the torrential rain. If he hadn't looked up at the cliff as lighting struck, he wouldn't have seen the opening at the end of the winding, narrow ledge. He most certainly didn't expect what he found in there.

JT's daydreams were interrupted when the door opened quietly behind him. Emma stuck her head out, looking up and down the hall. "Hi," she said. "Please come in. You are not going to believe what these gals have been through."

JT stepped through the door, closing it behind him. He turned to see Annabelle and Emily sitting on one twin bed, now fully dressed. JT stood speechless as Annabelle moved forward on the bed and Emma sat down in a chair.

"We were abducted, and Jean is evil," Annabelle blurted out. "She is a bank robber and totally evil."

"Yes, she is, and her brother is too," Emily added.

"Why didn't you say something?" JT asked.

"Well, JT," Annabelle replied, "you might have noticed she was always armed. And if I did say anything, you would have been the first one she shot."

Emily said quietly, "She also said that she'd torture us all to death afterward. And we believed her. She is evil, we all saw it."

Annabelle put her arm around Emily's shoulder. "We are safe now, and JT will protect us," she stated firmly.

"Yes, I will. But where is she?" JT inquired.

Emma, who had been quiet while listening to the nasty tale, leaned forward in her chair. "She tied and gagged these gals, then knocked them out. When she came downstairs, she told me she was going to the clothing shop and the bank."

"The bank?" JT exclaimed. "She was headed in that direction last time I saw her."

Emma stood up and said, "We need to get over there."

"Oh no, you two head to the doctor's. He needs to take a look at your head wounds. Emma, do you have a shotgun behind that reception desk?" he inquired.

"You bet. I wouldn't be without my trusted Greener. Never know when some drunk boarder is going to stumble over from the saloon and shoot up the place," she replied.

"Well, grab it and get these two over to the doc's. I'll see if I can catch up to Jean. She is probably long gone by now, but if she is as evil as you think there might be some people in mighty big trouble. You stay there 'til I come for you. I mean that," he said.

The women left, stopping briefly to fetch the Greener and some shells. JT stood outside and watched them head for DeWitt's office. Halfway there, Emma nodded to JT and pointed toward the bank. JT nodded and gave her a thumbs up. He hurried toward the bank, slipping the hammer strap off his Colt.

As he arrived, a gentleman with a small bank bag was trying the doorknob and rapping on the door. He turned to JT and exclaimed, "Something ain't right in there. There was a gal in the hallway a few minutes ago and it wasn't Millie."

JT stopped short. "Who's Millie?" he asked.

"Oh, she's the teller. Quite the looker, really," the gentleman said sheepishly. "Her dad runs the bank and I haven't seen hide nor hair of him either. His office is right down that hall," he said, peering through the glass.

"Where did the other gal go?"

"Right down the hall, I'm thinking she went out the back door. She looked like she was carrying something heavy."

"Well, the bank may have been robbed. I think I need to get in there."

"Oh my, I'll go get the sheriff," the man said and headed quickly toward the jail.

"Good idea," said JT, knowing very well that the sheriff was not in town. *Good to get him out of here; there's no telling what is going on in there.*

JT took out his Colt. Looking inside the lobby, he tried the door. It was locked. He pounded on it loudly and watched for any movement. He then turned his pistol and proceeded to smash out the small window above the doorknob. Using the barrel to clean up the remaining glass, he slowly reached inside and gingerly opened the door.

With his Colt cocked and ready, he surveyed the lobby and moved quickly to the end of the teller cage. He peeked around and breathed a sigh of relief as the narrow space proved to be empty. Turning his attention to the hallway, he crept to the first door and opened it. It turned out to be a janitor's closet.

From there, JT made his way to the office. Leaning down below any projected gunshot, he put his ear to the door and heard what appeared to be muffled cries for help, interspersed by sobbing.

He moved to the side of the door, slowly reaching out to the ornate brass doorknob. He twisted it slowly but it stopped almost immediately. *Locked,* he thought. "Hello, who is in there?" JT yelled. "I'm the sheriff and you need to come out with your hands over your heads." Seconds went by that seemed like an eternity, but all he heard was a muted cry for help, much louder this time.

JT backed up to get leverage in the narrow hall and delivered a solid kick to the door. It barely moved. "Stand away from the door," he shouted, then put three shots downward into the lock. With one more kick, the heavy office door opened.

Jean rode out of the livery stable with a sigh of relief. She put her untested horse into a gallop, heading back toward the trail she had come in on. She thought she knew where her brother Cain was going with his idiot friend Billy. She looked up at the dark and cloudy sky and thought, *I better get there before this rain comes.*

A long shot, she knew, as it was a day and a half away from where JT had shown up and ruined everything. If the rain held off, she could follow their tracks and give those two a piece of her mind for leaving her behind.

Money apparently meant more than blood to Cain, as he had saddlebags stuffed with money from the bank in Colby. *God damn that jerk, he just turned and got his butt out of there, without looking back,* she fumed. But she knew exactly where they were heading. On the outskirts of the small town of Lakeview, they had a cabin tucked deeply into the woods and she'd surely find them there.

JT rushed into the banker's office, gun leveled, anticipating anything. What he found was an attractive blonde draped across an elderly man who appeared to be not long for this world. The young woman was sobbing and screaming into a gag that was stuffed into her mouth. JT satisfied himself that there was no one else in the office and moved toward her.

"Relax," he said. "I'm not the sheriff but I'm a good guy. I'm going to cut you loose."

The woman, once freed, spit the gag out of her mouth. "Help me," she screamed.

"Yes, I will. Let me look at this fellow," he said, already knowing the banker was dead. He gingerly turned the man over and looked up at the woman. "I'm sorry, he's gone," he said quietly.

"Oh my God," Millie sobbed. "She killed him, she killed him!"

"Who did?" JT inquired.

"I don't know, I don't know. But she made my dad open the safe. She took some cash and some gold and left."

JT was faced with a dilemma. Jean was certainly the person this gal was talking about, and was probably only five minutes ahead of him. But what would he do with this young lady? He looked down at the sobbing woman and made his decision. "Let me fetch the doctor for him," he said quietly.

The young woman looked up. "No, you're right, he's gone. She killed him," she said, no longer crying. "Find her, please find her, and kill her!" she shouted.

"What is your name?" he asked her gently. "Millie," she replied. "OK, Millie, someone will be here shortly. I will catch the woman who killed your father."

As JT hustled toward the livery with his Colt drawn, he spotted Buck leading his saddled horses out of the barn.

"Hello," he called out. "Did you see a woman come through here? And why are you leading my horses?"

Buck turned toward JT, gesturing to the horses. "Well, a gal did come through here. She told me you were coming right behind her and I should saddle your horses. She took the horse you brought in, said it was hers. I hope that was OK?" Buck asked sheepishly.

"Where did she go?"

Buck pointed down the trail. "The same trail you came in on. And she had a message for you."

"Really, and what was that?"

"She said thanks for nothing."

JT gazed down the trail. "Damn," he uttered out loud.

"What's going on?" Buck inquired.

"Well that's kind of a long story. Let's just say she is an evil one. Did she tell you to saddle my horses?"

"You bet, she said you would be coming right along."

JT looked at the cloudy sky and his empty saddlebags. *I could go after her now, but she may be hoping for that, waiting to ambush me. If this sky opens up, I'm going to lose her tracks anyway,* he thought, as a raindrop hit the ground in front of him.

Making up his mind, he slid into the saddle. "Buck, do you have a rifle I can borrow?" he inquired.

"Sure do," Buck said. "Let me fetch it for you."

As Buck hurried back into the livery, JT was startled by a voice behind him. He drew his Colt and pivoted Pete toward the voice.

"It's just me," Annabelle exclaimed, hands shooting toward the sky.

"Whoa, you startled me," JT said, replacing his gun in its holster. "Why aren't you with the others?"

"They are in good hands with the doc. I was worried about you. Where are you going?"

"Well, Jean robbed the bank. She is getting away and I need to catch her."

Buck jogged out from the stable. "Here you go!" he yelled. "I brought you some extra ammunition as well."

"Thanks," JT said. As he reached down for the rifle and ammunition, the skies opened up.

Annabelle stepped under the stable's eaves and said, "Are you out of your mind? You can't track her in this rain. Besides, she is one hell of a shot. She'll take your head off if she gets the drop on you. Anyway, I think I know where she is going."

JT stopped. "Really?"

"Yes, I think so. I heard her and her brother talking about the cabin in Lakeview," Annabelle replied.

JT nodded. "OK, let's get the hell out of this deluge," he said as he nudged Pete and Re-Pete back into the livery. Looking down the trail, he thought grimly, *But I'm coming, Jean, you can count on it.*

Chapter Five

JT and Annabelle went to DeWitt's office, toweled off and wrapped themselves in blankets. Their clothes were on hangers, drying off next to a wood stove. Emma, Emily, and Dawn were already in the cramped room.

"What happened at the bank?" Emily asked. "Someone came to fetch the doctor right after Annabelle left and said someone was hurt at the bank."

"That's right," JT replied. "Jean did it. She robbed the bank and hightailed it over to the livery. She's gone, took off before I could get there."

"Well, now you know she's as bad as we said," Dawn replied. "What are we going to do about it?"

"You? Nothing. But I'm going to head out for Lakeview in the morning and there will be hell to pay for all of them," he said vehemently.

Annabelle moved forward on her chair. "Well, I'm going with you, and I won't take no for an answer."

JT looked at the woman and saw that there was no talking her out of it. He smiled. *Boy, mighty attractive with spirit to boot,"* he thought. "Well, if you insist, we will leave at dawn. Let's get dressed and I'll buy what we need at the mercantile store."

"I can come too," said Emily.

"No, you stay here and look after Dawn," JT replied. "The doctor is going to be busy and we are probably going to have a funeral. I think Jean killed the banker."

The next morning, JT and Annabelle had breakfast with the women. JT supplied enough money to last them a couple of weeks, though he hoped they wouldn't be away nearly that long. They bid the women goodbye with the requisite hugs and safe travel wishes.

As they walked by the jail JT noticed that the door was wide open. "Let's stop in here," he said, nodding toward the office. Inside, they found the sheriff asleep with his head on the desk. JT knocked loudly on the open door but the sheriff did not stir. JT knocked louder and yelled, "Wake up!"

With slits for eyes, the lawman slowly looked up. "What?" he said quietly.

"Are you the sheriff?"

The man looked around the room and put his hand on his chest, finding his badge in its place. "Yeah, I guess I am. And who are you?"

"I'm JT Thomas and this is Annabelle…." He glanced at her, realizing he didn't know her last name.

"Annabelle Hewitt," she stated.

"Well, what can I do for you?" replied the sheriff. "Can't you see I'm busy?"

JT snorted, "Yeah. So, did you have a good time drinking whiskey at the Stevens Ranch while the bank was getting robbed?" he said with a snarl.

The sheriff put his head back on the desk. "Yeah, I missed that." A few seconds later he was asleep again.

JT looked at Annabelle and shook his head in disgust. He looked around the office. It was neat as a pin. Everything was brand new, even the coffee pot and well-stocked gun rack above the new credenza. JT eyed a stack of wanted posters on a small table. "Let's have a look at these," he said.

Annabelle moved up next to him and yelped, "That's Jean's brother!" She took the stack and began sorting through the posters. "Here are the rest, even the ones you killed!" she exclaimed. "And here is one for Jean, my God!"

JT took the poster. "I'll be damned," he uttered. "She is wanted alive for bank robbery and larceny. $500 reward."

"How about the others?"

"Her brother is wanted dead or alive for $1,000. The others are $250, dead or alive as well."

JT took the posters and folded them up, looking down at the hung-over sheriff. "Well, if he had been doing his job, checking out the newcomers instead of getting drunk, maybe Jean would be in jail and the banker not at the undertaker's. Anyway, let's get on the trail. Times a-wastin'," he said firmly.

JT and Annabelle quickly made their way to the livery, where Buck made short work of saddling Pete and Re-Pete and a very nice gelding JT had purchased from him.

"What is his name?" Annabelle inquired, as she took her seat on the sturdy horse.

Buck smiled and responded, "Pete."

"Oh, very funny!" Annabelle exclaimed.

"Doesn't have a name, so you can name him," Buck replied, as JT laughed.

Annabelle turned to JT. "Let's call him Ready!" she said.

JT handed Buck an extra $100, saying, "You look after my girls, Buck. I'm counting on you."

Clenching the money over his head, Buck replied, "I'll treat them like family. You go and catch those bank robbers."

"I will," JT replied, smiling.

Chapter Six

JT looked up at the clear, sunny sky and thought about the woman he was riding next to. She was no doubt beautiful and smart, but there was something about her that he couldn't place. He felt drawn to her. She seemed a woman, not a girl, a woman that was comfortable in her skin. JT knew that was not easy to do out here.

The West was hard on women, though most were treated fairly well because there were so few of them. If they were married, they worked side by side with their husbands and were required to have as many babies as they could.

JT had heard the phrase "barefoot and pregnant." He didn't know about the barefoot part, as most women he met had shoes of some sort, even if they were old and worn out. But pregnant—absolutely. When JT looked at women walking down the wooden boardwalks in the frontier towns, he guessed that one out of four was pregnant.

Annabelle seemed different somehow. But brave and independent as she was, he felt the need to look out for her and keep her out of harm's way. He somewhat regretted agreeing so quickly to bring her along, since he just didn't know what was ahead of them. *Could be gunplay,* he thought to himself. *I'm going to need to keep her out of that.*

"How are you doing over there?" JT called out.

Annabelle, who had been lost in her own thoughts, nodded and turned toward JT with a smile. "Good," she answered. "And you?"

"Very good. I'm glad you came along," he said, regretting the statement even as it came out of his mouth.

Annabelle laughed. "Don't bullshit me. You had no choice and I'm guessing you are regretting the moment you agreed."

JT turned toward her, cocked his head and frowned slightly, with no response.

"Oh, come on," Annabelle insisted. "I've been watching you for the last two hours trying to figure out how to get out of this mess, Mr. Handsome Rescuer."

He shook his head and said, "I'm thinking Jean is headed back to where I ambushed them. We may pick up some tracks soon. Lakeview is a straight shot from there and I'd like to stop at the place I spotted you from. It's a cave and I left a few things there that I'd like to retrieve."

"A cave, really? I don't think I've ever been in a cave"

JT chuckled. "Well, you might like it. It's furnished!"

The weather was nice as JT and Annabelle made their way up to the narrow trail that led to the cave.

"Annabelle, the trail is very narrow and I'm not sure how Ready will handle it. So why don't you dismount and you can ride Re-Pete? He has been up and down and I'd sure feel better with him underneath you."

Annabelle looked over at JT. "That's a good idea. Shall we leave Ready here or take him along?"

"I'll tie him loosely to Pete and ride behind you. If he bolts, hopefully he bolts away from us. You may not want to look over the ridge; it's quite the drop-off."

"Naw, heights don't bother me, but thanks for the tip. I'm dying to see a furnished cave," she said with a broad smile.

As they made their way up the narrow trail, Annabelle commented on the beautiful view. "Yes, it's something to behold, but not at night in a downpour," JT said with a chuckle.

They finally topped the trail. Outside the entrance to the cave was a large flat surface with a huge boulder in the middle. JT swung around it and stopped their horses next to the opening. As they dismounted, JT motioned to Annabelle and whispered, "Let me go in first, you stay here with the horses. Don't unsaddle them just yet."

Annabelle nodded, taking all the reins and whispering in Ready's ear, "Nice job, boy."

JT pulled out his Colt and moved slowly toward the entrance, which was about twelve feet high and ten feet wide. He listened but heard no sound. Stepping inside, he crouched low and surveyed what he could see of the dimly lit cave. Seeing no threat, he hollered, "Come out with your hands up!" There was no reply, so he turned and walked back outside.

He pulled a lantern and a bottle of kerosene out of his saddlebags. Filling the lantern, he said, "We will leave the horses here for a bit, then come back and unsaddle them."

"Are we staying here tonight?" Annabelle responded.

"I think so, but that's up to you."

The couple made their way cautiously into the cave. As they moved farther inside, Annabelle gasped as she saw the chest of drawers, a dining set, and an armoire filled with what looked to be expensive china.

"Oh my," she gasped. "You weren't kidding. It really is furnished, with very nice pieces."

"Yes, the bed is back there, and who knows what else," JT said with a smile.

Annabelle turned around in a circle and walked back toward the cave entrance, peeking around it and viewing the narrow trail. Turning around and moving back toward JT, she said, "How did that miner get all this in here? That trail is too narrow and he must have had help."

"Boy, I hadn't thought about that, but you're right." He looked toward the rear of the cave. "Well, what should we do? Shall we get out of here or stay?"

"Oh, let's stay. It's kind of cozy and I'd like to check out the entire cave," Annabelle said with a smile.

"OK," JT responded. "I'll tend to the horses and get us some water. See if you can find wood for the stove and I'll bring in some supplies."

After unsaddling the horses and removing the saddlebags, he fed them some grain and told them he'd be back soon with water. He picked up a saddlebag and strolled back into the cave. Not seeing Annabelle, he called out, "Where are you?"

"Back here," Annabelle responded, just as she came out of the darkness with an armful of neatly split firewood. "You have got to see this!" she exclaimed, turning and disappearing into the darkness.

Dropping the saddlebags against the wall and turning up the lantern, JT carefully followed her. The cave widened to ten feet, and they stopped about twenty feet past the bed. The left side was dry and lined with expensive furniture, stretching back into the darkness. On the right side, he saw a line of water running down the wall and disappearing into a three-inch crack. But what really caught his attention was an honest-to-God bathtub pushed up against the wall of the cave, which was filled but not overflowing.

JT turned to Annabelle. "Doesn't this beat all," he exclaimed, pointing to pipes connecting the tub to the flowing water. One was filling the tub, the other dumping the excess water down the crack. Annabelle knelt down next to him, shaking her head in silent amazement.

Leaving JT kneeling at the tub, she moved out of sight behind an ornate room divider. "Well," she declared, "I don't think it beats this!"

As JT turned the corner he stopped, speechless. Annabelle was sitting on a pretty ceramic commode, next to a tin bucket. "Can't a girl get a little privacy while she does her business?" she said, laughing. She stood up and looked down into the commode, beckoning to JT.

JT moved tentatively forward, hoping not to find something disgusting. As he looked over the ornate commode ledge he chuckled wryly, "Now, this guy had some good ideas."

The bottom sloped from front to back with what looked to be varnished wood, cut exactly to fit the commode. Apparently, the bucket was for dumping water over the person's business and washing it away through the crack.

Annabelle stood and motioned at the cave walls. Every dozen steps there was a lantern hung on a peg. "All the comforts of home," she commented. JT shook his head at the audacity and creativity of the miner.

"Well, let's get back," he said. "I don't know about you but I'm starving. We will have plenty of time to explore in the morning."

"OK," Annabelle agreed. "I'll fill up the bucket; you never know when nature might call in the night," she chuckled.

"Let me do that," JT responded, as he grabbed the bucket. He knelt next to the constantly filling tub and smelled the surface. "Smells OK," he commented. He cupped his hand

and brought up a bit of water, then dipped his finger in it and tasted it with the tip of his tongue. He smiled up at Annabelle. "Water is fine, good for drinking. Or flushing" he said with a smirk. "I'll fill up the bucket for the horses first."

As they made their way back toward the cave entrance, Annabelle gestured to the bed. "What did you do with the miner's remains?" she quietly inquired.

"I made a cairn. It's too rocky for a burial," JT responded.

"Well, he had a nice bed. Maybe you should use it."

"Not me. You go ahead."

"Maybe I will, but that mattress is going to need to be flipped over. I'm not sleeping on the dust of a skeleton."

"Well, he didn't die on the bed. He was actually on the floor. And from what I could tell he was shot."

"Oh, my!" Annabelle exclaimed, holding up the light and looking for a potential shooter.

"I wouldn't be worried; the man killed himself. There was a gun on the floor and the skull was blown open from the under the chin and up through his brain. Besides, I found a suicide note that says whoever finds this note can have everything in the cave as long as we take care of the graves. There's also a reference to a diary, but I didn't see one."

Annabelle stood somberly and JT said quietly, "Why don't you see if you can get that stove started? I'll finish tending to the horses and bring in the tack and saddlebags."

"OK," Annabelle replied. "Speaking of saddlebags, whose saddlebags are those? And whose rifle is that?"

"Those are mine. I left in a hurry last time I was here," he said with a chuckle. "The miner's gun is in there as well," he said, pointing to the saddlebags. "That's one of the reasons I came back. The gun is like nothing I have ever seen."

As he turned and left the cave, Annabelle said to herself, "This is getting more interesting by the minute." She looked at the small cook stove off in the corner and frowned, turning around in a circle. She fixed her gaze on a fire pit in a corner near the cave entrance. It was surrounded by fieldstones and had apparently been used quite a bit.

"Let's cook over a fire. I'm not good around stoves," she said to herself as she gathered the wood.

JT stopped to admire the view outside the cave. The gun he had found next to the miner had slipped his mind. As he unsaddled the horses and gave them water from the bucket, as well as some more grain, he thought about the unique revolver he had examined while staying dry in the cave. It was a .45 caliber but had a very short barrel without a sight. The hammer was oddly shaped and long, probably built for fanning. The holster was also odd. It was cut away and made the gun easily accessible. When he tried them together, the holster seemed to make the gun practically jump into his hand. He started to feel comfortable with his new find and was looking forward to loading it and firing at a target or two. There was no manufacturer's stamp on the revolver, so JT surmised it was a custom revolver, obviously made with loving care and great skill.

He tethered the horses for the night and brought the saddles into the cave, noticing the fire. "Decided to forgo the stove?" he asked.

"Yes. I don't do well around stoves, and to be honest I'm not much of a cook," Annabelle replied.

"Well, let me get the rest of the stuff in here and I'll take a crack at cooking."

Annabelle pulled a couple of frying pans out of the saddlebags and added more wood to the fire. *And he can cook,* she thought with a smile.

Chapter Seven

Jean rode into the small town of Lakeview. It was familiar to her and, while the town didn't have a view of the lake, it also didn't have a jail or a sheriff. That is what attracted Jean and her brother to build a cabin outside of town, one which actually had a lake view.

She rode up to the only saloon in town, recognizing her brother's horse tied to the hitching rail. Sliding off her weary horse, she walked up the stairs, through the batwing doors and stepped to the side. The place was not busy at mid-afternoon, but there stood Cain and Billy, bellied up to the bar with a bottle of whiskey half empty in front of them.

Cain immediately noticed his sister in the mirror behind the bar. He did not turn around; rather, he motioned to the bartender for another glass. "Hey, sis," he said. "Come have a drink. Where you been?"

Jean strode briskly up to the bar, grabbed her brother's arm, turned him violently around and slapped him across the face.

"Where have I been? Where have I been? Are you kidding me? In the Godforsaken town called Point Stevens Pass, no thanks to you." She looked at the glass, picked it up, and thought about throwing the whiskey in his face. Sniffing it instead, she looked at the bottle. "What is this?"

"It's Scotch whiskey," Cain replied. "Try it, it's good."

Jean tossed the whiskey back with an experienced twist of the wrist. "Not bad," she commented. "Pour me another and explain yourself. How the hell could you leave me?"

Cain hung his head. "I don't know, it all happened so fast. I mean, heads were exploding, horses were falling, and I had no idea what was happening. I just panicked. I knew you would find us and I still have the money," he said, as he held up a roll of bills.

Jean grabbed the money and put it down the front of her shirt. Nodding to Billy, she picked up the bottle and turned toward the door. "Bring a few more of these; we are going to the cabin. We've got a bank to rob."

Annabelle woke to the aroma of coffee and saw JT at the fire pit. "Hello," she said quietly.

"Well, good morning," JT said with a big smile. "Been waiting for you to wake up 'cause I'm starving. I've got eggs ready to make and the bacon is almost done. I've got pan bread with peaches as well. How do you like your eggs?"

Annabelle rolled out of her bedroll with a smile. "My God, you do know how to cook!" she exclaimed.

JT chuckled. "Not so fast, you haven't tasted anything yet."

Annabelle put on her boots, stood up, and stretched. She motioned toward the back of the cave. "Well, I'm going to do my business," she said, picking up a lantern and the full bucket. She looked over her shoulder. "And I'd like scrambled eggs with bits of crispy bacon in them," she said with a chuckle, and disappeared.

JT laughed. "You got it," he said, and got busy.

"That was wonderful!" Annabelle exclaimed after breakfast was finished. "You really do know how to cook."

JT looked up. "Yes, my mother taught me, and my father was a pretty good cook as well. He said if you wanted to eat you needed to learn to cook."

Annabelle nodded. "That makes sense." Looking at the frying pans still sitting near the fire pit, she said, "I'll clean up, but let me do it outside in the sunshine."

JT looked over at her. "That would be great, and I'll bring the gear out."

After everything was cleaned and stowed and the horses were saddled, JT paused. "Well, do you want to explore the cave more or should we get going?"

Annabelle looked at the cave opening. "I'd like to when we have more time. Right now, let's not let Jean get away."

"All right, you're the boss," JT commented wryly, moving the horses slowly toward the trail.

Sliding up and into the saddle, Annabelle chuckled, "Well, I'm glad you figured that out."

The journey to Lakeview was uneventful and gave Annabelle lots of time to check out JT. They camped each night, with JT doing the cooking and Annabelle doing the cleanup.

JT practiced with the unique pistol, a hundred draws empty and twenty or so with bullets. Annabelle was impressed with his speed and accuracy.

On the last day, Annabelle took some small pieces of wood and threw them about five yards apart into a creek while JT stood with his back turned. When he glimpsed the floating pieces, he turned quickly and attempted to hit the targets. He missed the first two, but then went on to hit the next eight.

"Nice job," Annabelle said.

"Thanks," acknowledged JT. "First ones weren't so great, but I'm thinking I'm getting the hang of this gun. It's easier to shoot than my Colt, and it kind of jumps out of the holster."

"Are you going to switch?"

"I'm thinking about it."

"Well, why not use both? Slide your Colt to the left side, pull it out backwards and leave this one on your right side."

"Not a bad idea. So, how do you know about guns?"

Annabelle just smiled and headed back to camp.

JT and Annabelle pulled up in the hills overlooking Lakeview. JT took out his spyglass and surveyed the town. It looked to be a small place with a short main street, about a dozen establishments, and no boardwalk.

"Very few pedestrians, horses, dogs, or elephants," JT joked. Removing his rifle from the scabbard, he motioned to Annabelle to do the same. "Let's ride in slowly and see what we can see. You keep an eye on the rooftops and I'll pay attention to the street," he said.

Annabelle nodded without saying a word. She had a firm expression on her face and didn't seem to be afraid at all. JT nudged Pete gently in the side and said, "Let's go." Annabelle nodded again and moved up alongside him.

As they rode into the little town, JT noticed there was no jail or bank. There was, however, a saloon. They rode up and down the street but, catching no sign of their quarry, they dismounted in front of the saloon.

"You best stay here," JT said firmly.

"Women aren't welcome in there?" Annabelle asked.

"Probably not, unless they serve food. I want to see who is in there."

"I understand. I'll wait here and keep my eyes peeled."

JT walked up the steps and quietly opened the batwing doors, stepping to the side with his hand near his new gun. A cowboy seated in the right corner was working on a glass of rotgut. Two cowboys sat at the bar drinking beer. The bartender was standing behind the bar with a frown on his face, drying off a glass. JT moved up to the bar.

"What'll it be?" the bartender asked.

"Just some information," JT replied.

The bartender turned around and headed toward the beer tap, filling up the glass he had been wiping. He moved in front of JT, setting it down gently. "First beer, no charge for a new customer. On the other hand, information is not cheap," he said with a smirk.

JT picked up the glass, tilted it back, and proceeded to down it all at once. He set it back on the bar, looking the bartender in the eye. "Well, the beer is warm but that glass is surely clean," he commented wryly.

The bartender chuckled, "It is at that."

JT took out the wanted posters and put a $10 gold piece on top of Jean's. The bartender looked up and put up two fingers. "Two posters, twenty bucks," he said.

JT put another coin on the bar, holding it down with his middle figure. He looked up at the bartender. "Well?"

"Yeah, I've seen 'em both. They were here a few days ago, but I haven't seen 'em since," he said.

JT took his finger off the coin. "Is that unusual?"

"Yeah, now that I think of it, it is. They live in a mighty nice cabin out on the lake and there ain't much to do around here.

We serve some pretty good grub and neither one of that bunch can cook worth a damn." He looked over at the cowboy in the corner and yelled, "Ain't that right, Gordon?"

Gordon looked up. "Who you talking about?" he replied, belching.

"Cain and your girlfriend Jean," said the bartender. "Fat chance," he said to JT under his breath. "Jean don't like the boys much."

"Where can I find this fancy cabin?" JT inquired.

"Easy to find. Head out northwest; it's less than a mile from here and you can see the lake before you get there. They even got a sign up where you turn off."

"Oh, that's handy. What's the sign say?"

"No trespassing," the bartender said with a straight face.

JT turned toward the batwing door as Gordon stood up, wobbling. "Hey, I heard what you said, and you ain't going to hurt Jean," he grumbled, moving his hand toward his Colt.

JT stopped and looked at the drunken cowboy. "Whoa, take it easy. Who said I'm going to hurt her?"

"Don't bullshit me, I know she's wanted and you're just a damned bounty hunter, aren't you?"

JT paused. "Well that's possible, but you see she robbed a bank and hurt some nice people, may have even killed one."

"I don't give a shit. You reach for those guns and I'll tell Jean I killed me a bounty hunter that was looking for her."

"Knock it off," JT murmured, just as Gordon went for his gun.

"Oh shit," he uttered and juked to the left. He picked up a bar chair and threw it at the inebriated cowboy. Gordon, apparently seeing double, fanned a few shots at JT, missing by a mile. JT reluctantly pulled his Colt from its new position on his left side and winged the right arm of his antagonist.

"Ouch, ouch, ouch, holy shit, that hurts!" Gordon cried as he dropped to the floor, tossing his gun and holding his injured shoulder. He tried to sit back up. "Boy, am I drunk," he muttered as he passed out and slid toward the floor.

JT looked at the two other cowboys. "Guess he was."

He turned toward the door, surprised to see Annabelle standing inside the batwing doors.

"Most people would have simply killed him," she said, then turned to leave the saloon. "You are a good egg, John Thurgood Thomas."

JT replaced the spent shell in his Colt. "She sounds just like my mother," he chuckled as he turned and followed her out.

Riding down a long trail that led to the cabin, JT nudged Pete past the "No Trespassing" sign. *Well, that's unfriendly. How about some barbed wire, too?* he thought. Pulling up a hundred yards from the cabin, he signaled Annabelle to dismount.

"Let's leave the horses here and reconnoiter," he said.

"Reconnoiter," Annabelle commented, "My, my, someone must have been in the army."

"Oh yeah," was all JT said as he moved into the woods and quietly headed for the cabin. It was on a hill facing the lake, with a wide deck around it and a well-worn path leading up to it. JT took out his spyglass, surveying the back and the one side he could see.

"Can't see much from here," he said quietly. "Let's move toward the lake and get an angle from there."

Annabelle whispered, "OK. Notice, no windows in the back or sides."

JT nodded and gave a thumbs up as he led them through the dense woods. As they got closer to the water, JT heard a slap behind him and stopped briefly.

"Damn mosquitos," Annabelle mumbled under her breath. "I hate mosquitos!"

JT chuckled and kept moving toward the water. Stopping at the water's edge, he surveyed the lake side of the cabin with his German-made spyglass. The deck was unoccupied and there were large windows looking out over the lake.

"Very pretty spot. What's the name of the lake?" Annabelle whispered.

"I think I heard the bartender call it Cranberry."

Seeing no cranberry bushes, Annabelle grunted. "Really?" she asked.

"Yeah, I know there aren't any cranberries in Colorado. Maybe it's the shape of the lake."

"Oh, well why didn't they just call it Round Lake?"

"Heck, I don't know, maybe it was already taken."

JT continued looking through the glass. "Boy, no movement up there and I can see into the windows quite well."

Annabelle looked toward the cabin. "Well, these mosquitos are driving me nuts."

"OK. Let's head toward the back and take a listen."

With Annabelle slapping and cursing, they approached the back of the cabin. JT handed Annabelle his rifle. "You stay here, I'll reconnoiter," he said with a chuckle, moving toward the front of the cabin and under the deck.

He took off his hat, drew his Colt, and peeked over the railing, looking directly into the cabin. There was no sign of movement, so he made his way up the deck stairs, ready for anything. Sidling up to the nearest window and peeking inside, he spotted no one and heard nothing. JT moved to the end of the deck, put his ear to the door, and tentatively turned the doorknob. It wasn't locked.

He slowly opened the door, assuming the unlocked cabin must be occupied, and stepped lightly through the door, paying special attention to the open doors inside. He could see a couple of beds and a chest of drawers in one room, but no napping bank robbers. Moving over to the other room, he listened and heard nothing there either. He then stepped briskly inside, gun drawn. The room was empty.

JT moved out onto the deck and hollered, "Annabelle, all clear!"

She stepped up the stairs quickly. "So, no one's here?" she asked.

"Not unless they are having a party in the outhouse," he replied snidely, pointing to a small shack in the woods.

"Well, shit, no pun intended. So, where are they? They weren't in town. If they're not here, where could they be?"

"Damned if I know," said JT, watching the sun begin to set. "How about we fetch the horses and stay here tonight? There was no place in Lakeview to stay, except maybe the back rooms in the saloon. And for that, I'd have to sneak you in and dress you up like a whore!"

Annabelle smiled. "Not likely," she said as she made her way down the steps and headed toward the horses. "Beats fighting the mosquitos," she said over her shoulder.

Once the horses were taken care of, JT scrounged up some food from the cabin, cooking by candlelight. Annabelle was sitting on the deck in the dark with a rifle, keeping watch for any returning bank robbers. JT was sipping on some excellent whiskey he'd found. He tapped on the window, gesturing to Annabelle to come in for dinner.

"Thank God!" she exclaimed. "Those mosquitos are driving me crazy out there."

JT had moved the small table into the corner and had the meal set out, ready to be consumed. Annabelle sniffed the air and said, "Smells wonderful."

JT blew out all of the candles but one. "Great," he said as he sat down. "Let's eat."

The meal finished, JT nodded toward the dishes. "We can clean up in the morning," he said. "We need to take shifts and keep watch; there's no telling if and when they are coming back. I'll do the first, so take a nap if you can. I will wake you up when I get sleepy."

He put his rifle and his Colt on the table and chuckled to himself.

"What's funny?" Annabelle asked.

"Oh, that just made me think about my grandpa Emil. He was the king of naps. The man lived to eighty-two years old, and he attributed it to naps, a daily ration of good brandy, and all-night Saturday poker games," said JT.

"Really? He sounds like a wise man, or at least a fun one."

"We called him GGP and we all loved and looked up to him. He was exceedingly respectful of women, and was always preaching about attention to detail, as he was a tailor by trade. He also was a crotchety, critical, judgmental old man who didn't suffer fools but wasn't prone to prejudice. In fact, his shop assistant Lester was a black man. GGP said Lester was his best friend and the finest man he had ever met, apart from being the best tailor he had ever been associated with. Mr. Lester actually made a lot of my clothes when I was growing up, and gave me pretty high standards for what I wear to this day."

Annabelle smiled. "You know, I think that's the first time you ever told me about your past life. In fact, it's probably the most you've ever said about anything!"

JT chuckled. "Well, that's all you get for now. Now get some sleep!"

Morning came quickly. Annabelle stretched, yawned. and greeted JT, who was still up after the last watch.

"Good morning," JT said. "I've checked the surroundings and it's all clear."

Annabelle frowned. "Well, what do we do now?" she asked.

"As for Jean and Cain, I wish I had a good answer for that," JT replied. "For now, it's back to Lakeview. I'll go in to see if the barkeep has any news, then we will head back to Point Stevens Pass."

Annabelle nodded. "Mind if I come in with you this time? Never hurts to have somebody watching your back, you know. Besides, I feel silly standing out in the street."

JT smiled. "Not a bad idea. We probably never will be back there anyway, so the heck with 'em if they don't like it."

Chapter Eight

Tying their horses outside the Lakeview saloon, JT and Annabelle passed through the batwings and moved toward the bar. The bartender started to say something, but JT sliced his finger across his throat and put his hand on his Colt. As they worked their way to the bar, Annabelle looked around and gave JT an elbow to his left side.

"Ouch!" JT exclaimed, looking down.

"That's Billy in the corner," she whispered, motioning to the scruffy long-haired fellow at the corner table. "He's Cain's friend and one of the gang that captured us!"

They strode up to the bar and JT put down a $20 gold coin, then turned and looked directly at Billy. With him was the hung-over Gordon. Both men were engrossed in their breakfasts until Gordon looked up, locked eyes with JT, and froze.

Billy eventually noticed Gordon and turned toward the bar to see what he was looking at. He put the flapjack into his mouth, chewing slowly with his mouth open, spitting pieces onto the table.

"Well, who do we have here?" he said, looking at Annabelle. "Did you miss me? You know I always wanted a piece of you, but that bitch-loving Jean wouldn't allow it. And here you are! I'm beginning to think there is a God."

JT stepped in front of Annabelle. "Didn't your mother ever teach you how to chew with your mouth closed?" he asked with a smirk.

Gordon whispered in Billy's ear and pointed at JT. "Well, she tried," replied Billy, "but I killed her right after I slit my father's throat. Gordon here says you shot him without giving him a fair chance. What was that all about?"

JT chuckled. "He was drunk and I gave him a break. Now you, on the other hand, not so much. Especially after what you just said about your mom and dad."

Billy stood up, throwing his napkin down on the table. "Oh, I've killed lots of folks, including some kids. But that was after I raped and had my way with them. Nothing like a feisty woman that fights you right up to the end," he said with a smile. "And I'm gonna kill that red-haired whore standing next to you after I've had my way with her, just as soon as I kill you."

"Get out from behind me and sit at that table," JT said over his shoulder to Annabelle. His gaze shifted between the two men across the room.

Gordon stood up next to his friend and said, "I'm having a piece of you too."

JT chuckled. "Wouldn't have it any other way. We can bury both of you in the same pine box. By the way, you might want to take the strap off that poor excuse for a Colt."

Gordon did just that as Billy went for his gun, thinking JT would be distracted. JT pulled his unique pistol and turned sideways. Billy's shot went right to where JT's heart had been a second ago.

JT was a hair slower but his aim was true, and Billy was hit in the chest above the heart. He looked up at JT. "God damn, I thought I had you," he said, as he collapsed to the floor.

In the meantime, JT fanned a shot at Gordon, who was leveling his Colt, and hit him in the middle of the stomach. Gordon dropped his gun and fell to his knees, folding over and clutching his belly.

JT nodded to Annabelle, signaling her to stay put. He moved up to Billy, who was still holding his revolver. JT took it and looked down.

"Well, I think you're dead, asshole, but this one is for your dad," he said, putting a slug into Billy's chest. "And this one is for your mom, may she rest in peace," he said, putting a slug in the middle of Billy's forehead.

JT glanced at Gordon, who was clutching his stomach. "My God, that hurts!" Gordon cried. Looking up at JT, he said, "Just shoot me."

JT looked at the bartender who had witnessed the entire confrontation. The bartender shrugged his shoulders. JT then looked at Annabelle and she nodded. "He is in pain; he'll die within the hour," she stated firmly.

JT nodded, knelt down next to Gordon and whispered in his ear. He stood up and waited as Gordon said a prayer. Gordon finished, looked up at JT and nodded, and JT put a bullet above his nose.

Annabelle stood next to JT as he replaced his spent cartridges. "What did you tell him?" she inquired. "Well, I told him to make peace with the good Lord, that he was a good guy, and I was sorry it didn't work out with his girlfriend," he said.

Annabelle smiled and put her arm around JT's broad shoulders. "I knew you were a good egg!" she said.

JT laughed. "My mom thought so too," he chuckled. "My dad, not so much."

Turning to the bartender, JT motioned him over. "Billy has a $250 bounty on him. If you want to take him to a town with a sheriff, you can have it."

The bartender nodded. "Well thank you, I will, and in spite of that crack about the pine box I'll even bury Gordon and pay for a headstone."

JT nodded. "Yeah, he seemed like an OK guy, just got mixed up with the wrong crowd, especially the wrong girlfriend. Have you seen Cain or Jean since we were in?"

"No, haven't seen hide nor hair of them."

"Any idea where they might have gone?"

"Well, if they ain't at their cabin then I'm guessing they are out robbing a bank. That's the only thing Cain is any good at, except drinking my expensive booze," he said with a laugh. "They'll be back to the cabin eventually, though, unless someone kills 'em first."

JT turned to Annabelle. "Let's get out of here," he said.

"Where to?" she asked.

"Back to Point Stevens Pass, maybe with a quick stop at your favorite cozy cave. That place intrigues me."

"Me too," Annabelle said quietly.

They mounted up in front of the saloon and turned toward their destination. Annabelle nodded at the gun on JT's right side. "So, how did that work out?"

JT looked straight ahead. "Well, it damn near got me killed and I just got carried away. I have been thinking it's a pistol that's used in competition. That's why I turned sideways, since that's what they do in those damn things. Lucky thing too, 'cause he would have plugged me for sure."

Annabelle nodded. "Yeah, I saw that. So, what are you going to do?"

JT nudged Pete, moving forward quickly and looking over his shoulder. "I'll just have to keep practicing."

Chapter Nine

Cain shook his head as he watched his elder sister riding erect and effortless in the saddle, eyes straight ahead. She had always been a good rider and a better sister. Cain was nine years old, living on a small farm in Ohio when his mother and father just up and died. He heard it might have been something called dysentery, but he really didn't know. All he knew was that his sister stepped into the breach.

After burying them in the field behind the small farmhouse, she saddled his father's prize horses, put saddlebags on the plow horses, and loaded up every canned good in the house. Cain remembered what followed as clear as if it were yesterday. Jean moved the horses back and away from the farmhouse, picked up a large canister of kerosene, and mounted the steps.

As she looked all around her, Cain thought he saw tears run down her face. Then she turned and walked into Cain's only home and proceeded to slosh it thoroughly with kerosene. She backed out, spreading the smelly liquid around the porch, then dropped the can and moved to where the horses were saddled. She told Cain to say goodbye as she struck a match and dropped it onto the kerosene.

For a while, they lived above a saloon in a small room. Cain knew Jean spent a lot of time downstairs at night cozying up to the drunken cowboys. He didn't know what she was doing with them, as she never brought them back to their room.

But he heard the bartender talking to patrons in the bar as he emptied the spittoons and swept the floor, saying that Jean was the best whore in the joint. He didn't know what that meant at the time, but he knew she was keeping them fed, warm, and dry.

As Cain grew, he developed a habit of sticky fingers. He often dipped into the till when the bartender wasn't looking. He also became quite adept at shoplifting, to the point where they were banned from most of the stores in the many towns they frequented.

Cain smiled to himself as he remembered how they stumbled onto bank robbing, quite accidentally. Jean had a good week with the cowboys and they stopped in the local bank to deposit her earnings. She explained that there was no place to hide money in their room, so the bank was the best bet.

While they were standing in line, waiting for the only teller, the short man in front of Jean pulled out his gun. He stuck it in the teller's face and announced, "This is a stickup. Raise your hands above your heads and no one will get hurt."

He motioned to the teller to empty the till into a bag he had brought with him. Turning toward the door, he spotted the bag Jean was holding above her head. "I'll take that too, little lady," he said with an evil smile.

Cain laughed at the memory. Without missing a beat, Jean had brought the heavy bag down on the short man's head. He stumbled back into the teller's cage and dropped his revolver on the floor. Cain immediately reached down, scooped it up, and pointed it at the teller. "Hands back in the air," Cain ordered. "This is a stickup again."

The original bank robber had straightened up, pressing his left hand to the growing knot on his head and holding the bank bag tightly.

"Give it to me," Cain snorted. The man shook his head and said nothing. "I'm not asking again. Do it now," Cain said as he reached for the bag.

The man saw an opening and lunged for Cain's gun. Cain pulled the trigger, shooting the man in the stomach. He folded over and dropped to the ground.

Jean took the gun away from Cain with a frown on her face, just as a banker moved from the rear of the bank where he had been hiding. Jean turned the gun on the man and put a bullet just under his nose. Looking down, Jean saw a small derringer in the dead man's hand.

Jean turned and pointed the revolver at the teller. "You can put your hands down," she said. The teller did so with a hint of a smile. "Sorry about that," Jean whispered, and shot him in the forehead.

The only person left was an elderly woman who was shaking with fear. Jean said nothing as she shot her in the chest.

Jean gestured to Cain, pointing to the back of the bank and the rear door. Cain nodded, stopping to pick up the derringer from the banker's hand on the way out.

The original bank robber was moaning and clutching his stomach. Jean knelt down and looked the short man directly in the face. "You know what, pal?" she uttered.

"No, what?" the man whispered, obviously in excruciating pain.

"That was FUN," she hissed, putting the gun directly on his forehead and ending his misery. "Sure beats whoring," she said to no one, with a wicked smile.

She moved quickly to the rear entrance where Cain was waiting. "Let's get the hell out of here," Jean said as they stepped through the doorway. Pointing to the livery, she began to undo her buttons, revealing a small but noticeable amount of cleavage. "Liveryman is a customer of mine. I'm sure he will be glad to see me," she laughed.

Cain snapped out of his daydream as Jean pulled her horse to a stop and pointed at a copse of trees near a tiny winding stream. Looking at the sky, she said, "It's early, but this is where I told Billy to meet us. I sure hope he did what he had to do, whatever that was."

Cain hoped that "whatever that was" hadn't gotten Billy killed since he was bringing their supplies for the trip and they needed him for this next bank job. Billy was quick on the draw and quicker at losing his temper, and it was bound to be the death of him.

Cain slid off his tired horse. They would make do with what they had, and maybe Jean could catch a trout or two in the little creek. Quite the fisherman, she loved to gut and behead the fish. But this was just one of the many abilities Cain admired about her.

The next day, they slept late and had a quick breakfast of coffee and hardtack. They didn't expect Billy this early, so Jean used the time to practice with her rifle and Colt. She was a crack shot with the rifle and she could snake that Colt out quicker than a rattler. She was scarily accurate as well. *A God-given talent, I guess,* Cain mused. *Or maybe a devil-given talent.*

Afterward, Cain was stretched out on his bedroll, with the back of his head on his saddle and a half-empty bottle of whiskey in his hand.

Jean took a swig out of her canteen and looked at the sky, saying, "Billy should be here in a bit. I'm going to scout around and see if I can scare up a rabbit or two. That jerky just didn't do it for me. If he shows up, fire three shots into the air and I'll come a-runnin'."

Cain raised the bottle with his right hand and gave her a thumbs up with his left.

Hours later, they hadn't seen a trace of Billy. "Where the heck is he?" Jean asked.

"Maybe he got drunk with Gordon," Cain replied with a frown. "You know how they like to drink."

E. Alan Fleischauer

Jean looked at the whiskey bottle. "Look who's talking," she said scornfully. "If he ain't here by morning we head out to Point Stevens Pass. The gold in that bank is calling me!"

Cain smiled and rolled over, dreaming of gold, whiskey, whores, and more gold.

Chapter Ten

The journey back to the cave was filled with conversation. JT was a bit surprised to find out that Annabelle was in fact married and had a teenage daughter.

"My daughter Madeline lives on the east coast with her father. She's a beautiful and talented actress and singer, and I miss her very much," Annabelle said with a sad smile.

"My husband Marcus is a handsome, charming man who gave me no indication of what a narcissist and womanizer he actually was. His father was a doctor; a noble, quiet man who was like a father to me. I assisted him with his patients, and he promised to send me to what he jokingly called 'The doctor school.' He used to say I was a better caregiver than he was, especially my bedside manner."

Annabelle frowned. "Everything changed when his wife died. She had been a pillar of the community in New York, wealthy beyond anyone's dreams. One day, she just keeled over while having tea with her book club, and he lost all interest in life. He stopped seeing patients and friends and started drinking a lot."

"Marcus became isolated too, and moved to another bedroom in the house. He began to stay out all night and smelled of alcohol at breakfast in the morning, if indeed he did show up. Things went from bad to worse after I caught him cheating on a regular basis," she said with a hint of anger.

"I talked about getting a divorce but he wouldn't hear of it. So one day I just packed a bag for Maddy and myself and took off for points west. Unfortunately, Marcus' henchmen caught up with us at a roadside inn. They took Maddy by force and left me with just the clothes on my back and no money."

"Thankfully, the innkeeper and his wife took pity on me. They gave me a job cleaning rooms during the day and waiting on the customers in the tiny restaurant and bar. It was hard work, but I saved a bit from tips and wages. After six months, I had enough money to purchase a one-way ticket for a stagecoach ride to St. Louis. It was a long dusty journey, with customers and drivers being replaced in every town, but I enjoyed the freedom of it. It also gave me time to realize I'd married too soon."

Annabelle gave a small smile and went quiet. JT nodded. *This woman has been through a lot,* he thought. *No wonder she seems so strong.*

JT caught a whiff of rotting flesh near where he had rescued the women. *Horse and human,* he thought. He skirted the area and kicked Pete into a canter. Annabelle followed suit.

As they approached the trail to the cave, they slowed down their mounts. JT motioned to Annabelle to follow behind. Sitting high in the saddle, he kept his eyes peeled as he rode up the winding narrow trail. They found the cave entrance looking the same as before; no horses were tethered outside and no bank robbers were lazing in the sun. They brought in their supplies, bedrolls, and saddles.

"Would you like to explore the rest of the cave?" Annabelle inquired. "It seems a bit early for supper."

"Well, that's why we came," JT replied. "No time like the present." They lit lanterns and JT led the way.

Walking by the bed, the still-full bathtub, and the out-of-place commode, JT laughed loudly. He stopped at the first lantern hanging on the wall and took it down gingerly. "My God, it's full," he said. "Wick looks good too. Let's see if it works."

He pulled a match from his breast pocket and fired it up. As he followed the passage and lit the rest of the lamps, they passed by a seemingly endless row of furniture. Annabelle stopped and reached out to touch an exquisite, ornate desk. "My, gosh, look at this. It's beautiful!" she said, pulling the sturdy desk chair out.

"Ah, how about we come back to this? I'd like to get to the end of this thing, if it has an end," JT said wryly. He turned and moved toward the end of the cave.

Annabelle got up, running her hand over the desk. "I think you're holding some secrets, my friend," she murmured.

They continued on, passing piece after piece of furniture. "Did you notice?" Annabelle said as she touched JT's elbow.

"What's that?" JT replied.

"These pieces are ALL wonderful, he didn't bring back just any piece. And think of all the time it took! Also, I'm looking around and I'm not seeing any sign of mining."

"You may be right. Hey, I think I see daylight ahead! Let's keep going."

JT stood at the cave's rear entrance, looking at the sunset in the canyon below. His hand was on a large buckboard that was in pretty good shape, despite all the years. There was a clear trail gradually leading down to the canyon. It was wide enough for the buckboard.

Annabelle showed up at his side. "Now we know how he got the furniture up here. Also, there has to be a way out of that canyon," JT said. He watched as dusk settled over the canyon, then turned and said, "Let's get back."

Annabelle glanced to the other side of the entrance and stopped, seeing two crosses planted firmly into the rocky ground, one cross larger than the other. She walked over and read the names carved into them. JT quietly moved up alongside her. "Joanne and Angie," he said.

Annabelle took JT's left hand in hers and squeezed lightly. "Well, he had help, didn't he," she said quietly, as she bowed her head in prayer.

JT nodded and lowered his head, taking off his hat.

Jean woke up at dawn, hungry and angry. Cain was curled up and snoring in his bedroll, sleeping off the effects of his liquid vice. She looked over at him and re-lit the smoldering fire.

She let the horses drink their morning fill, then brushed and saddled them, chatting with them as she did. "That damn Billy, I knew we couldn't count on him. Probably got himself and Gordon killed," she said with a sigh.

She rolled up her bedroll and put it behind her saddle, then moved to her sleeping brother. Kicking him on the bottom of his boot, she said in a singsong voice, "Wake up, wake up, sleepy head."

Cain stirred and started to turn over. "Oh, no you don't," she said firmly. Setting the coffee down next to the fire, she moved to Cain's horse and grabbed his canteen. Standing over his legs and looking down at his puffy face, she slowly poured some of the canteen's contents into his open mouth. She jumped away quickly as her little brother sat up straight, choking and gagging.

"What, what?" he yelled.

"Time to rise and shine, little brother. Coffee is ready, go do your duty and let's get out of here." Cain looked around, shaking off the water and sleep.

"Where's Billy?"

"He ain't coming, brother. It's just me and you, just like the old days."

"Well, more for us big sister, more for us!"

Cain headed toward the creek to relieve himself. "Let's go rob a bank!" he yelled at the heavens.

Chapter Eleven

Cain and Jean pulled up outside of Point Stevens Pass. Jean picked a spot in the trees, far enough away that they couldn't be seen by any passersby.

"What's this town like?" Cain asked as they finished making camp.

"Small but pretty nice," Jean said. "You're going to see it right quick, though, 'cause we need to supply up and I certainly can't go in there!"

"Yeah, I figured. What do you need me to get?"

"Here is a list. Get yourself some rock candy if you like; I don't want you drinking 'til this is over. And no stopping in the saloon!"

"Yes, Mommy," he replied and mounted up, slipping the list into his pocket and waving his hand as he headed out.

God, I hope he'll be OK, Jean thought, frowning as she watched his retreating figure.

Cain rode down the main street with his hat covering as much of his face as possible. The jail's door was open and he could see the sheriff sitting at a deck with his hat over his face, apparently taking a little siesta. He stared straight ahead as he rode by the bank, the saloon, and up to the mercantile store. Nobody seemed suspicious or particularly aware of him. There was a drunk sleeping it off in front of the saloon, a few women going in and out of shops, and one fellow going into the bank clutching a bag.

He slid off his horse and led him to the water trough in front of the mercantile store, pulling his hat down over his eyes. Once his horse had drunk his fill, he stepped briskly up the steps.

There were a few customers in the shop. The clerk nodded at him while taking care of a pretty young lady with her back to him, putting her purchases in a box. "How is it going at the bank, Millie?" the clerk inquired.

"It's going all right," she replied. "But gosh darn, I miss my dad! I never knew how much work it took to run a bank."

"Yes, your father was a good man, but hang in there, Millie. You're smart, you can figure it out."

Millie nodded, smiled sadly, and picked up the box. "Maybe, maybe not," she said as she headed out the door.

Cain handed the clerk his list. "Couldn't help overhearing; that gal runs the bank?" he asked quietly.

"Yes, and she is in over her head," the clerk whispered. He perked up as he looked at the list. "I'll get these things for you. There is a nice selection of hard candy over in the glass case," he said with a wink.

Cain smiled weakly. "Great. Put that stuff in a couple of bags. I'm on horseback, no need for a box."

Cain paid up and stepped down the stairs, putting most of the supplies in the saddlebags and hooking the remainder in the bag over his saddle horn. He looked around, not spotting any of the women they had held captive, then pulled his hat

down low and rode slowly down the street. He had nearly made it past the saloon when he groaned to himself and said, "Aw, just one."

He stepped through the batwing doors and moved to the bar. "Beer and a bottle of good whiskey," Cain said with a smile.

The bartender frowned. "That'll cost you extra. Good whiskey ain't cheap.

Cain pulled out a wad of bills and threw it on the bar. "How's that, Mr. Barkeep?"

"Yes sir, good whiskey and a beer coming right up. First beer is on the house for a new customer!"

Cain smirked. "Thanks. Say, do you have any scotch back there?"

"You bet, it's in the back room. Don't get much call for that, but you got plenty of money and I'll fetch it for you!"

Cain had made his way through half the bottle of scotch when two dusty drifters pushed through the doors. They separated and stood against the wall on either side of the door. Satisfied that there was no one that could be a challenge, they moved up to the bar. "Whiskey," they said in unison.

The bartender reached under the counter, pulled out a bottle of rotgut and filled two glasses, which were quickly emptied.

"Fill 'em up again," one of the drifters uttered.

"That's two bits each. Show me your money," the bartender stated firmly.

"Oh, we ain't got no money," the drifter said. He looked over at Cain and the expensive bottle of scotch. "Hey, how about you share?" The drifter's partner pulled his Colt and leveled it at Cain.

"Whoa, take it easy, I'll give you a drink. In fact, take it all," Cain said as he slid the half-empty bottle down the bar.

"We'll take that money roll too," said the drifter, pointing his Colt the money on the bar with an evil smile.

Cain quickly slipped his revolver out of its ornate holster and drilled the dusty drifter in the middle of his chest.

The dying man looked down, dropping his Colt on the floor. He reached up to cover the hole, trying to stop the red gush of blood that was quickly soiling his shirt and pants. "Shit," he said, as he dropped to the floor.

The partner had his gun leveled at Cain. *Oh no,* Cain thought, not in a position to respond. But as the man began to pull the trigger, his head exploded, scattering flesh and brain. His body stood erect for a moment, headless, then seemed to take a step toward Cain, collapsing in a bloody heap.

Cain looked at the bartender, who was holding a smoking shotgun. "Thanks," Cain said quietly.

The bartender nodded. "I've had this since I started tending bar here. Never had to use it before," he said. "Gotta protect my paying customers."

"Well, I'm glad you did. You saved my life," Cain replied. "I guess that's my cue to get back to camp," he said, just as the sheriff walked in the door.

"What the hell is going on?" asked the sheriff, as he pointed his Greener at Cain.

Cain raised his hands after sliding his Colt into his holster. "Hey," the bartender exclaimed, "it ain't his fault." He explained to the sheriff in excited detail what had happened.

"OK, put your hands down, Mister, you're free to go," the sheriff said. His eyes fell on the bottle of scotch. "You mind?" he asked.

"Help yourself," Cain replied as he turned toward the door. "It's all yours."

The bartender yelled after him. "Hey, you forgot your money!"

"Keep it," Cain said over his shoulder, walking out and waving his hand above his head. "You earned it!"

The sheriff continued to help himself to the scotch. "You need to help me get these bodies to the undertaker," he said to the bartender.

But the bartender wasn't listening. "Dang," he exclaimed, "there must be close to a thousand dollars here!" He looked at the sheriff. "What did he do, rob a bank?"

The sheriff paused before finishing his whiskey. "Maybe I should look through those wanted posters," he said.

Chapter Twelve

JT woke up early and started a small fire from the embers. Once he had coffee ready, he made a cup and held it under Annabelle's nose. Her eyes opened and she smiled. "Good morning, that smells good."

"Well it's for you, sleepyhead," JT replied, handing her the cup. "I'm going to tend to the horses and then get breakfast started." He turned toward the cave entrance.

After breakfast and cleanup, they lit lanterns and continued exploring, moving past the ornate furniture. Eventually, the passage ended in another opening to the outside. Exiting the cave into the daylight, JT looked down the slope.

"You know, I'm going to bring Pete out here and check out that canyon. Looks like some good grass down there." Looking back at the mountaintop, he said, "I see a stream running down the mountain. That must be where the water in the cave comes from."

"Do you want me to go with you?" Annabelle asked.

"Naw, I won't be long," JT replied.

They turned back into the cave. Annabelle stopped at the large desk, turning the lanterns on the cave wall up to their maximum. "I'm going to check out this magnificent desk while you are gone," she said. JT nodded and continued down the tunnel.

Annabelle ran her hands over the desk's smooth surface, then picked up her light and moved away, slowly moving past more incredible pieces. She thought *These weren't picked up from random wagons. I think they came from one source!*

Annabelle returned to the desk as JT called out, approaching with Pete. She said, "JT, you be careful out there. I think I'm warming up to you, cowboy."

JT chuckled. "What's not to love?" he replied.

Annabelle looked up, smiling. *Love? Love, maybe.*

JT rode Pete down the slope, stopping occasionally to admire the view. He could see the small creek coming off the mountain behind him; fields of grass, pines, and spruce dotted the landscape. Large and small boulders could be seen next to the canyon's edge.

He rode down to the mountain stream, checking out the hoof and paw prints. He recognized tracks from deer, elk, a cougar or two, various small critters, and a few large horses. Looking back up the hill and catching a glimpse of the back end of the buckboard, he thought to himself, *Hmm, maybe the miner's horses managed to survive.*

After a while he began to worry about Annabelle being left alone, so he decided he would head back after letting Pete drink his fill from the stream. JT dismounted and pulled his canteens off his saddle horn, bending down to refill them.

Pete pulled his head out of the stream, sniffing the air. JT capped his canteens and quickly remounted, leaning down to pat his friend.

"What is it?" JT asked just as he heard a whisper of a growl. Turning toward the sound, JT was faced with the largest bear he had ever seen.

Pete reared and backed up into the stream, turning in a circle until JT grabbed the reins. "Stop, easy, Pete," he said as calmly as he could. He slid his Sharps out of the scabbard as the bear stood up on its hind legs, looked at the heavens, and let out a growl like a thunderclap.

Pete reared on his hind legs, throwing JT into the shallow stream, and bolted off toward the cave. With his head under water, JT clutched his Sharps and looked up at the blue sky, which now had bubbles in it. The bear roared at the retreating horse, dropping to its feet and starting to give chase.

JT broke the surface of the water, sputtering and choking. He dug his feet into the stream bed and held tightly onto the Sharps. He hit the slope of the stream on the opposite side just as the bear turned around, giving up on the bolting horse.

JT moved the Sharps into his left hand and removed the hammer strap from his Colt. The Sharps had one cartridge in its chamber. Laying his Colt on his stomach, he wiped his eyes with his right hand and quickly gripped the rifle with his left as the bear leaped into the stream. Its yellowed jaws were wide open, and putrid saliva dripped off its mouth. The devil was in its eyes.

JT aimed his Sharps as well as he could and hit the bear in its upper chest. The bear hit him, burying him with its stink and girth. JT turned his head into the river bank, grabbed his trusty Colt, and emptied it into the stomach of his vile opponent.

My God, I can't breathe, he thought, as he saw the sun disappear under the fat and fur of the angry animal.

Back in the cave, Annabelle started at the top of the desk. She slowly pulled the first drawer open, taking it out and putting it on the desktop. She sorted through the contents, not finding anything interesting. She replaced it and opened the second; it was empty.

She opened the third drawer and nearly dropped it as she brought it to the desktop. It contained a red velvet bag that filled the drawer. Picking it up, she murmured, "My, my, that's heavy." The bag was tied tightly, and it took effort to get it open. Once she succeeded, she was amazed to discover it was filled with diamonds.

She emptied the bag into the drawer and spread out the gems. There were all sizes, including a few uncut stones. Annabelle turned up her lantern and picked out one of the largest. "Oh, my!" she exclaimed, "this must weigh over four carats."

She sorted through the rest briefly, holding the gems to the lantern light. Finally, she carefully put them back in the bag, anxious to open the next drawer.

It was then that she heard the Sharps. Standing up, she quickly replaced the bag and moved toward the cave entrance. It was then that she heard JT's Colt firing in rapid succession. "Oh, no!" she exclaimed, hurrying to the entrance.

Emerging into the sunlight and looking below, she spotted Pete and the largest bear she had ever seen. It was sprawled half in and half out of the water. JT was nowhere in sight. She started down the slope, watching the bear that appeared not to be moving. "JT, JT, where are you?" she shouted.

She moved into the canyon and slowly made her way toward Pete. "Come here, boy," she said quietly. Pete did not move, pawing at the ground. Gripping the horse's reins, she patted him on the side of the neck. "Where's your master?" she asked. Pete nodded his head up and down and took a tentative step toward the bear, which was obviously dead. "JT, JT!" Annabelle cried out again.

She reached up and took JT's Winchester out of the scabbard, noticing that the Sharps was missing. She pointed the rifle at the bear and moved slowly, prepared to shoot. As she walked through the stream, she thought she heard a muffled voice saying, "Help me! Get me out of here!"

Annabelle walked around the bear. She spotted the tip of a boot sticking out from under it. "JT, it's me," she yelled, as she dropped to the ground.

"Thank God. Get me out of here, I can't breathe," replied JT in a weakened voice.

Annabelle's nursing skills kicked into overdrive. Moving quickly, she took the lariat off of Pete and looped it under the left foreleg of the bear's carcass, then placed the rest of it around its head. She tied it tightly and knelt back down.

"I'm going to move the bear off you. Are you hurt?" she asked.

Annabelle listened but there was no response. Moving briskly toward Pete, she took a second to calm the jittery horse before climbing up into the saddle. Tying the lariat on to the saddle horn, she began backing JT's trusty horse away from the stream.

Pete, who had been on more than one cattle drive, steadily moved backward, slowly turning the dead bear over onto its back, half in and half out of the stream. JT wasn't moving as Annabelle slid out of the saddle. "Good boy, Pete," she said, as she quickly made her way back to JT.

Even before she knelt down, she saw that he was breathing. The back of his head and neck was a scratched bloody mess. Gently turning him over, she felt his legs, arms, and chest. "All right, looks like no bones are broken," she whispered.

Looking at the slope, she pondered how she was going to get JT back into the cave. Hotfooting it back up the slope, she slipped inside the cave and grabbed a well-used axe that was lying next to a woodpile. Quickly making her way down the slope again, she thought about her time with the Cheyenne. She had made a travois numerous times and she was about to do it again.

Checking on the unconscious JT, she made quick work of felling the outside of the travois, slicing JT's lariat into short sections to bind the pieces together. She did the same with the smaller cross sections, then laid pine boughs across the sled. Pete stood stoically as she hitched the contraption to him, then moved him across the stream and right next to JT. With effort, she lifted him head first onto the travois, then tied him down and started slowly up the hill.

She led Pete into the cave, where she clumsily moved JT off the travois and laid him in on the bed. She stripped off his clothes and did a perfunctory job of wiping the blood off him. Then she brought Pete back outside, took the travois off, and moved the water pail near enough that he could drink. "Nice job," she said as she patted him on the neck.

She retrieved JT's medicine bag, then picked up the blankets from his bedroll and made her way back to the bed. Spreading the blanket over the naked JT, she smiled approvingly. *What's not to love*, she said to herself.

Pulling up a chair, she gently turned him over on his side, taking the time to thoroughly clean his wounded head and neck. Thinking she needed to stitch up the deeper wounds, she decided to wait for better light as she spread salve on him. As she repacked the medical bag she sighed, exhausted. She gently crawled over JT, snuggled under the shared blanket, and fell off to sleep.

Chapter Thirteen

Jean was stir-crazy and nearly starving in camp while she waited for Cain's return. She had cleaned her weapons three times, wondering if she shouldn't take a chance on shooting a big fat rabbit. She watered the horses and rubbed them down, a job that she hated and normally left to the missing Cain. She suspected he'd stopped for a drink or eight and was passed out in the saloon or, worse yet, in a jail cell. "Well, I can't wait here forever," she grumbled, picking up her saddle.

"Hello the camp," came a familiar voice as Cain rode in.

Throwing her saddle on the ground, Jean picked up a stick from the fire and threw it at her brother. It hit his horse in the rear flank and he reared in panic, throwing Cain to the ground. Jean stalked up to her disobedient brother and kicked him in the back and ribs as he curled up in a ball.

"Ow, ow, ow!" Cain wailed. "Stop it!"

"Where have you been?" Jean exclaimed.

"In town. I brought some grub, and I got good news."

"Well, it can wait 'til I've eaten. God damn it, go fetch my food. I'm starving," she said as she threw wood on the fire and took out a frying pan.

When the meal was done, Jean glared at Cain and said, "OK, so what's the good news?"

"Well, the banker's daughter is running the bank, and I was told she is in over her head," said Cain.

Jean nodded. "Doesn't surprise me. She's mighty good looking but she ain't smart. So, what the hell did you do?"

"Well, I got our supplies and then stopped for one drink," Cain said, hanging his head.

"One drink, my ass; you're still drunk. We hit the bank tomorrow evening, so get a good night's sleep."

After a hearty breakfast of coffee, bacon, pan bread, and peaches, Jean sat her baby brother down next to the fire and reviewed their plans.

"Here is how this is going to go," Jean said. "We go in after dark and we wait till the sheriff makes his early rounds. We'll slip into his office while he is gone and we will be waiting for him when he returns. You stand behind the door and I'll be sitting at his desk. Stick that Colt of yours to his head but don't kill him!"

"OK, OK," Cain replied. "What next?"

"I'm going to walk the sheriff over to where the teller lives, then we'll head over to the bank. I want you to take all the horses behind the bank and tie them up near the back door, then head to the boarding house. That kerosene you bought is going to come in handy," she said with a smirk.

"What do you have in mind?" Cain inquired.

"I want you to burn it down," she said with an evil smile. "Soak the outside walls and the lobby, then torch the place. Then you hightail it over to the bank and wait for me to come out the back door."

"Why burn it down?" Cain objected.

"Why? Because I want that cowboy and those bitches to suffer before they die."

Cain nodded, frowning. "OK, you're the boss."

"Yes, little brother, I am. Now unpack the horses. We are going to need all the room we can get for the gold."

After a late supper, they mounted up and headed to Point Stevens Pass, arriving at dusk. Looking through the barred window of the jail, Jean signaled a stop. "I don't think the sheriff is in there. Let's hide these horses, then go back and get the jump on him," she said.

The sheriff finished his dusk rounds and opened the door to the jail, thinking of an early drink at the saloon before a late supper. As he stepped through the door, he felt the muzzle of a pistol against the back of his head and heard the telltale cocking sound. Cain reached around, removed the sheriff's revolver, and unloaded it.

Jean stood up and moved away from the windows, motioning the sheriff into his chair. The sheriff immediately recognized both of them, having sorted through his wanted posters last night. "Hey, you're Cain and Jean Cantrell!" he exclaimed.

"Yes, nice to meet you," Jean replied. She took the sheriff's pistol and signaled Cain to leave. "We need your help, sheriff," she said, handing him his empty Colt. "Get up and holster that thing. We are going to visit my favorite teller. I'm sure she'll be surprised to see me! Now lead the way."

JT opened his eyes in the dim light of a lantern. He looked over at the sleeping Annabelle and tried to sit up. Waves of nausea made him quickly lay his head back down. Reaching behind his head, he touched his neck and came away with blood and salve. He lifted the blanket covering him and was totally surprised to find he was as naked as a jaybird.

"Well, hello. It looks like you're going to live, big guy," Annabelle whispered.

"Holy cow! What happened?" JT asked.

"Don't you remember?"

"No…I don't, well I don't think so. I was dreaming about a bear, the biggest damn bear I've ever seen!"

"That wasn't a dream, big guy. You had quite the tussle with a big one. It darn near smothered you."

JT looked down. "Where are my clothes?"

"They are here but they need to be washed. They are soaked with bear blood!"

"So, you undressed me?"

"No, the dead miner did that," Annabelle said with a smile, as she crawled over him. "Do you have some extra clothes?"

"Yes, in my saddlebags."

"Well, I'll go fetch them. We can't have you walking around naked, can we?"

"So, you saw me naked!"

"You bet I did! I'm a nurse after all, but all I can say is…big guy!" She walked away with the lantern to fetch his clothes.

JT tried to sit up again and was pleased that the nausea was gone. He looked through the dim light, wondering how Annabelle got him back to the cave and onto the bed. *Quite a woman, quite a woman,* he thought.

Annabelle returned with JT's spare clothes. "Can you get dressed or should I help?"

"I can do it," JT replied.

"OK, then you do that, and I'm going to fetch something," she said and headed toward the desk.

JT struggled but finally got his clothes on as Annabelle returned, holding a red velvet bag.

"Well, you did it," she said as JT finished buttoning his shirt. "Can you walk?"

JT nodded.

They slowly made their way to the cave entrance, where Annabelle helped JT sit down. She covered him with a blanket, sat down next to him, and held out the colorful bag.

"What's this?" he inquired.

"Open it, but be careful," she replied, passing the bag to him.

"Heavy," JT said as he untied the velvet bag and glanced into it. With a quizzical look, he reached inside and pulled out a diamond, holding it up to better light from the cave's entrance. He looked at Annabelle. "Is this what I think it is?"

"I think so," Annabelle whispered.

He shook out a small handful of diamonds. "My God, there must be over a hundred here!" he exclaimed.

"At least," Annabelle replied.

JT looked at Annabelle and smiled. "And the miner and his family are dead, aren't they?"

"Why, I do believe so."

"Then I guess you are rich!"

"No, partner, we are rich, beyond our wildest dreams. You're the one who found this cozy cave, and it's even cozier now!"

Cain pulled the large canister of kerosene from his saddlebags after leading the horses to the back of the bank. He slowly approached the boarding house, glanced into the lobby, and saw no one at the desk. He gently opened the door, moved surreptitiously into the reception area, and drenched the desk, draperies, and staircase. Moving outside, he doused the deck and stairs, then the base of the house. A hissing tabby cat bolted out of the flowers, giving him a start. Cain, not an animal lover, stepped back.

"Whoa, get the hell out of here or I'll roast you," he said as the cat disappeared into the night. He returned to the front with a frown on his face. He actually liked the gals, especially Dawn. "But Jean's the boss," he murmured as he lit the smelly liquid.

He watched the fire creep up the stairs and around the base of the boarding house. Throwing the can aside, he hurried as quickly as he could to the back of the bank. Looking over his shoulder, he yelled "Fire!" as loudly as he could, hoping that Dawn could hear him and get out.

With Jean off to the side, the sheriff knocked on Millie's door. Millie parted the curtains and was surprised to see the lawman. Opening the door, she said, "Sheriff, what's going on?"

He hung his head and replied, "The bank is going to be robbed. Can I come in?"

"Yes, please," she said and moved out of the way.

The sheriff entered, with Jean moving in quickly behind him. "Oh my!" Millie exclaimed.

The sheriff shrugged. "I'm sorry, she got the drop on me."

"Hi, remember me?" Jean said with an evil laugh.

Millie stared in horror. "I certainly do. What are you doing back here?"

"Oh, I couldn't stop thinking about all that gold in your vault and…voila! Here I am!"

"Well, it's not…" the sheriff started.

"It's not what?" replied Jean.

Millie discretely shook her head at the sheriff. "It's going to take more than you to carry it. As you know, it's heavy."

"Oh, pretty girl, don't worry about that. You just lead me to it and you won't get hurt," Jean replied as she brandished her Colt. "Lead the way."

Emma was lying on her bed reading and dozing after a long day in her gardens. She sat up and sniffed the air. "Kerosene," she said to herself as she looked around for her cat. "Did you knock that lantern over again, Allie Cat?"

She got up from the bed, put her slippers on, and snugged her robe around her. As she opened the door to the reception area, she almost gagged from the fumes. Looking through the windows, she thought she saw movement beyond the steps. Then the stairs were lit with a bright glow that moved quickly up and through the open door. She looked up at the figure in the yard. He was throwing something away and turning abruptly toward the street, yelling "Fire!"

Then the curtains exploded in flames. She looked at the staircase, which was already engulfed, and thought about her guests. Emma added her voice to the cry of "FIRE, FIRE, FIRE!" as she backed away from the burning reception area into her bedroom. She quickly donned clothes and muddy gardening boots.

By now her bedroom window was also engulfed in flames, so she picked up her heavy desk chair and threw it as hard as she could through the glass panes. She quickly wrapped herself in her favorite quilt, said "Help me, Jesus," and then boldly threw herself through the burning, jagged window.

The sheriff and Millie opened the bank door, followed by a nervous Jean. Millie turned to the sheriff, asking, "Did you hear someone yell fire?"

"Yes, I did," he replied.

Jean shut the door and quickly locked it. "Oh, that's just my helper. He will be here in a minute or two. He likes gold as much as I do, so lead the way!"

Millie did so and opened the door to her father's office. Moving inside, Jean looked around. "Looks familiar. Oh, by the way, what happened to dear old dad?" she inquired evilly.

Millie stopped. "You killed him, and I will never forgive you for it!"

"Aw, wasn't me," Jean replied. "Looked to me like he had a bad ticker," she said with a chuckle. "Now open that safe and you won't get hurt."

"Sure, why not," Millie said with a smile. She spun the lock and quickly opened the safe. Standing back, she laughed and beckoned Jean to look inside.

Jean moved past the sheriff and Millie. She stood frozen. "Where…is…the gold?" she asked.

Millie quickly snatched the sheriff's revolver and pointed it at Jean. "It's on the way to Fort Collins with all the cash," she replied. "I sold the bank."

Jean looked at the gun in Millie's hand. "So, what's with the gun? Are you going to shoot me down in cold blood?"

"Oh yes. Just watch me," Millie replied, and pulled the trigger.

The Colt clicked. Millie pulled the trigger again and again as Jean stood with a smirk on her face. "You really think I would have left that gun loaded?" she said, then raised her Colt and fired two shots into Millie's chest.

She turned the Colt on the sheriff. "Well, I was going to have you help carry the gold, but what good are you now?"

The sheriff raised his hands. "I won't tell anyone about this, I promise!" he pleaded.

Jean leaned forward and looked the sheriff directly in the eyes. "Yeah, I believe you," she said, and shot him between the eyes. "Or maybe I don't," she chuckled, as she reloaded her revolver. Looking down at Millie's body, she said to herself, "What a waste."

Chapter Fourteen

JT woke up in the cave entrance, propped up on his saddle for a pillow. After a fitful night's sleep, he sat up sweating, shaking his head to clear it of the nightmare that seemed to persist even in the daylight. In his dream he had been drowning, pursued by a creature in the water. He fought and tried to get to the surface, but as he approached it, the creature pulled him back.

The cave entrance was filling with sunshine and Annabelle was curled up on her bedroll, breathing deeply with a smile on her face, still clutching the red velvet bag. JT looked at her and smiled. *She is something. I'm going to fall head over heels if I'm not careful.*

JT stood up gingerly, lit the lantern, and moved to the commode. The back of his head, neck, and shoulders hurt whenever he moved, but his nausea was gone and he could walk, though somewhat stiffly.

He returned to find Annabelle sitting up with a smile on her face. "Good morning," JT said.

"Well, good morning to you, big guy," Annabelle smiled.

"I feel well enough to fix breakfast if you will help a bit."

"Well don't push it, but sure, I'll help. I'll just be a minute and we can do it together," she said, heading for the commode.

As they ate breakfast, Annabelle said, "I need to stitch up the back of your head. That bear really did a job on you. I also have a poultice I have prepared for you."

JT nodded. "Hey, you're the healer."

She proceeded to stitch up the wounds. JT sat silent as a mouse with a grimace on his face. Then Annabelle reached into the fire and extracted a small piece of wood with a large ember burning at the end. She sprinkled a small amount of the herb poultice on the ember. She held her hands over the burning ember as the smoke and fumes rose, receiving the heat and the odor on her palms. Annabelle then looked out at the sky and uttered *'Mat to' wat'* as she spread the poultice on JT's head and back.

She stepped back to survey her handiwork. "Nicely done, if I do say so myself."

"Well, I'll take your word for it, unless you have a mirror," JT replied with a smile. "What did you say and do with the fire and the embers?"

"Part of the poultice is made from dried leaves. I said *'Mat to' wat,'* which means 'to burn the leaves' in Cheyenne. I was actually an assistant to a Cheyenne healer whose wife had died. He knew some English and recognized the word "nurse" when I was captured. So, he took me under his wing and taught me a lot about healing" She smiled at the recollection. "He kept the bucks off me, told them my red hair meant I was a witch who would turn them into a roaming empty spirit if they ever…," she said, laughing.

"Well, witch or not, thanks for your help," JT said.

"My pleasure, big guy."

"Hey, what's with all the "big guy" stuff? I'm tall, but not big guy tall."

"No, you're not so tall, especially when you're hidden under a brown bear," she replied. "But you are a big guy!"

JT shrugged and looked at the furniture. "Say, what else might be hiding in that desk? Did you have time to search it?"

Annabelle looked up. "Not nearly enough. I was thinking about that myself. Why don't we clean up here and check the rest of it out?"

JT nodded and set about the cleanup while Annabelle rolled up the bedrolls. Afterward, they headed back to the desk, lighting the lanterns on the wall as they went.

JT said, "Why don't you see what's in this desk? I'll check out the rest of the other pieces."

He began with an armoire that was made to hold dishes and plates. The top shelves were bare, but when he opened the bottom doors the dishes were there, carefully wrapped. A few of the dishes were broken but most of the others were intact. JT looked at the broken pieces and admired the handiwork.

The next was a chest of drawers, in which he found nothing of value except towels, sheets, and a tablecloth. After that was another armoire that looked like it was made to be placed in a corner. It was triangle shaped and the top was empty.

Opening the door, JT found carefully wrapped bottles. He unwrapped one to reveal a full bottle of cognac.

"Well, well!" he exclaimed. "Now that's more like it." The other bottles held more cognac and some red wine.

He moved on to a chest of drawers. The top two drawers were filled with woman's clothes and the bottom was filled with socks and a cigar box. JT smiled. He didn't care for cigarettes or chewing tobacco, but he was known to enjoy a cigar, especially while drinking a bit of brandy.

Wondering why cigars were hidden with women's clothes, he opened the cigar box. Lo and behold, there was nary a cigar in the box. It was filled with jewelry and currency. JT picked out an ornate necklace and held it to the lantern. It was linked with what looked like small gold sleigh bells. He shook it, and it gave off a delightful sound.

JT put the new find back into the box and headed back to Annabelle. On the way, he grabbed a bottle of wine and a bottle of brandy and, with the cigar box tucked under his arm, he whistled a catchy tune.

Annabelle was still seated at the desk and didn't notice him approaching. She had the lantern on the desk and seemed to be intently reading something. JT moved up behind her and cleared his throat loudly. Annabelle nearly jumped up out of the chair. "Oh my God, you scared me!" she said.

"Sorry about that. But wait 'til you see what I found!" JT exclaimed.

Annabelle smiled and held up the book she had been reading. "Wait, let me tell you," she replied. "This is the miner's wife's diary, and he wasn't a miner at all. He was a woodworker and an inventor. I haven't read it all, but the entire family came over to America, the last of their clan. They were Jews and came over to escape persecution in the 'old country.' They were led by the patriarch of the family, who was apparently a very talented jeweler. There's something about a brother being a gunsmith, and a duel. They were on their way to California when the Comanche attacked them. Only these two escaped and found this cave."

"But that's not the best part. There's a mystery here. The desk has a secret compartment! It says here, 'The keys are long and it takes two for you.' I think it's a clue!" she exclaimed.

JT shook his head. "Amazing story," he said. "You ready for my surprise now?"

Annabelle noticed the bottles and the bag. "What do you have there?"

JT grinned. "Oh, just a little refreshment and a fortune in jewelry. Want to celebrate being even richer?"

Emma rolled through the flaming window, landing in the yard and throwing off the burning quilt. Her wrists were cut, but just superficially. Moving to the front of the boarding house, she was not surprised to see her neighbors in the yard.

Some had buckets of water, but the fire was so intense now that no one could get close enough to do any good.

"My God, Emma, are you OK?" one of the neighbors asked.

"I think so, but I have guests in there!" she replied.

"Oh no!" the neighbor exclaimed as the roof proceeded to collapse.

"Oh God, Dawn and Emily are in there!" Emma wailed.

"No, I'm right here," came a voice from the crowd. Emma turned toward the voice as Dawn and the doctor approached.

"We were having a late dinner," DeWitt said.

"But Emily is in there!" Dawn exclaimed.

"Oh my God," he murmured.

Emily had fallen off to a light sleep, smiling after watching Dawn get ready for her dinner with the good doctor. She didn't smell the kerosene, and since her large room had no windows, she could not see the flames surrounding the house. She sat up straight when someone yelled "FIRE," then raced toward the door and poked her head out. The hall was full of smoke and the window at the end was engulfed in flames. The reception area was being consumed by fire, which was making its way down the hall.

Emily slammed the door and looked around the smoky bedroom. She started to cough uncontrollably and dropped to the floor. Looking up at the ceiling, she gave a start. It also was engulfed in flames. She crawled toward the closet, pulled on the hanging clothes, and grabbed the rifle from the back of the closet. With her back to the rear of the closet and her legs extending out into the smoke-filled bedroom, she cocked the rifle and put the muzzle in her mouth. She bent her head to pray. "God forgive me," she said resolutely.

Just then the ceiling collapsed, pinning her legs with a burning beam. Emily screamed and lost her grip on the rifle. She had never in her life felt so much pain. Surrounded by choking smoke, she found the rifle again and put the muzzle back in her mouth. With a final scream, she pulled the trigger. Outside, the crowd looked up at the sound of the shot.

"May she rest in peace," DeWitt murmured.

Emma looked at the smoldering remains of her boarding house with tears streaming down her face. She slowly collapsed to the ground and wept, curling into a ball and ignoring all that went on around her. DeWitt knelt and gently pulled her back up.

"Let's get her to my office," he whispered to Dawn.

Jean stuck her head outside the bank's rear door. Cain was seated on his horse and had his rifle out.

"Put that thing down," Jean declared.

"What was all the shooting about?" Cain said.

"They double-crossed us. There is no gold, no nothing!"

"No gold, you kidding me?"

"Do I sound like I'm kidding? She sold the damn bank!"

"What were the shots for?"

"Well, we have one less banker to worry about and the sheriff has taken his last drink! Let's get the hell out of here."

"Where to?"

"Home to Lakeview. Sheriff's dead and there ain't going to be a posse. Hell, we didn't even rob the damn bank!" she said, as she turned the horses toward the trail.

Chapter Fifteen

JT and Annabelle moved to the front of the cave. "What's in the bottles?" Annabelle asked.

"Brandy and some sort of red wine," JT replied.

"Let me see the wine. Hmm, nice stuff! I don't really drink much but I might have a little of this!"

"Sounds wonderful to me. I was thinking a little party is in order. We don't have much food left, but I think I can whip up something tasty."

After taking care of the horses and stoking the smoldering fire, Annabelle looked at JT. "How are we going to open this?" she inquired, holding up the wine bottle.

JT chuckled and went to his saddlebags. Rummaging around, he came back and showed Annabelle a shiny new knife.

"What is this?" she inquired. "I've never seen one quite like this before."

"That, my friend, is an *Offiziersmesser* army knife, which is now being used by the Swiss Army. I picked it up from a tinker who drove a hard bargain. But look," he said, as he opened the strange knife. "It has a corkscrew! That's what the tinker said, anyway. Now if I can just figure out how to use it," he said, blushing.

"Well, give it a try!" Annabelle said. "Office-reza-messinger or whatever you called it is a silly name. I'm going to call it a Swiss Knife!" She paused. "No, a Swiss Army Knife."

"All right, forevermore we christen this a Swiss Army Knife. Now let's see how it works!"

With a bit of a struggle, JT opened the wine. Annabelle sniffed it, saying, "Smells OK to me, but hold on." She went to the armoire and opened a door. She turned around, flourishing two beautiful wine glasses. "Voila!" she exclaimed.

JT poured a bit into Annabelle's glass and waited. "Aren't you going to try it?" she asked.

"Ladies first," he replied.

Annabelle proceeded to take a small sip, then a larger sip, and smiled. "It's wonderful!" she exclaimed. "Try it."

JT smiled and did so. "Very nice! But I think I'd prefer the cognac," he said, eyeing the unopened bottle.

"Well, more for me!" Annabelle exclaimed.

After an ad hoc dinner that Annabelle declared to be excellent, they sat around the fire, smiling and thinking about their good fortune. JT twirled his cognac in his newly discovered snifter and said, "Well, as my mother would say: Annabelle, you are a good egg!"

Annabelle almost choked as she laughed. "A good egg!" she exclaimed.

"Oh yes," JT responded. "That is her highest praise!"

"Well, thank you, Mom!" Annabelle laughed. "Yes, I know the term. In fact, I think I called you a good egg as well. You know, I had a mom too!"

"Yes, well to Annabelle Hewitt and John Thurgood Thomas, the good eggs," he said as he reached out to toast, clinking the glasses.

Annabelle looked up into JT's handsome face. She leaned over and kissed him lightly on the lips. JT leaned forward, putting down his glass. He put his arm behind Annabelle's head and pulled her gently forward. He kissed her back, then looked into her eyes.

"Well, I've wanted to do that for a while," he said and kissed her more intensely.

Annabelle stood up, picked up the lantern and beckoned JT to follow her. As she got to the bed, she turned into him and put her arms on his shoulders. "Well, I've wanted to kiss you as well. And more," she said, kissing him gently again.

"I'm glad to hear that. I started falling for you the day I met you, but I wasn't sure how to handle this, you being a married woman and all," JT replied.

"Well, I haven't seen my husband for over five years. He won't let me have a divorce even though I want one. I haven't been with a man since I left him," Annabelle said.

JT stared into her eyes. "What would you like to do now?"

She looked up, put her hands on his handsome face, and kissed him with gentle passion. "I'd like to make love to you,

JT Thomas, here and now." She stepped back and disrobed. Turning to the bed and drawing back the covers, she slipped into it. "Your turn," she said.

"Yes, it surely is," he said, as he slowly removed his clothing and slipped into bed. Annabelle snuggled into him and kissed him on the neck. Looking at JT's naked form, she smiled and giggled. "Hello, big boy."

Jean and Cain took their time getting back to the cabin since the sheriff in Point Stevens Pass was dead and no one had seen them almost rob the bank. As they entered, Jean spun around and went into the bedroom. She emerged quickly.

"Someone has been here, slept in my bed, and eaten our food," she said, as she looked at the clean dishes on the counter. "Heck, they even cleaned up after themselves!"

"Well, maybe some of the guys did it, Huck or his kid brother the Sandman. You know how I forget to lock the door," he said sheepishly.

Jean glared at him. "Yeah you do, but those jerks wouldn't have cleaned up after themselves." She opened a cabinet door. "And they would have drunk all your whiskey."

Cain nodded in agreement. "Well, who could it have been?"

"I don't know. Let's get settled in here and head for the saloon. Maybe that no-good bartender can give us an answer. Not much gets by him," Jean said.

JT woke up with a smile on his face and a slight hangover. He looked down at his bedmate in the dim lantern's glow, thinking, *This woman is something. My mother would say she is a good egg, but she would also call her a keeper, in spite of the husband and the daughter. And maybe she is.*

He got up, dressed, and went outside to tend to the horses and his morning duty. Returning to the cave, he stoked the fire, made what little coffee and bacon they had left, and brought a steaming cup to Annabelle. She got up and sat down next to the small fire. "How are you?" JT inquired.

"Good, I think," she replied. "I'm not used to drinking, so I'm a little bit queasy and have a nasty headache," she said softly.

"Your first hangover? Well, the coffee ought to help. Unless you want some hair of the dog…?"

Annabelle groaned and shook her head, slowly.

By morning, everyone in Point Stevens Pass had heard about the loss of Millie and the sheriff in an attempted bank robbery and Emily's death in the fire. Millie's death was keenly felt, especially so soon after the loss of her father. They offered sympathies to the strangers on the loss of their companion. No one cried about the sheriff, whose body was loaded unceremoniously into a wagon and sent to the Stevens ranch.

Emma woke abruptly on a cot in the doctor's office, with a soft pillow under her head and covered with a quilt. It was dawn, and sunlight streamed through the window. She sat up and looked around. She had been dreaming of her home burning down.

As she looked around at her surroundings, she realized it was not a dream. A tear rolled down her pretty, stricken face. *How could this happen?* she wondered. She had no enemies, and people seemed to respect her.

She roused herself and tiptoed out of the doctor's office. It was early and the few people out and about murmured their regrets and hurried on their way. She made her way to the burned-out shell of her former home, stood in front of the smoldering embers, and shuddered.

She felt chilled and hugged herself, shaking her head sadly. What was she going to do? There was no insurance; no one had fire insurance except those wealthy ranchers. She had less than a hundred dollars in the bank. Thank God she didn't have a mortgage; the smelly mess in front of her was all hers. Perhaps the land could be sold, but in the meantime where could she stay? A hotel for a month, perhaps, but what then? She shuddered again, holding herself tightly.

JT cleaned up after the meager breakfast and began to saddle their horses. "We are out of food and unless I shoot something we are going to starve to death," he said, looking at the hung-over Annabelle. "Can you ride?"

"I guess I'll have to, judging by the sun. Best fill up all the canteens; I'll need the water," she said.

She packed the jewelry and the diary in their saddlebags, thinking of the ornate desk and the potential mysteries it might hold. As JT led the way down the narrow trail, she anticipated coming back. *Soon*, she thought, *soon*.

On the trail, JT reflected on the past few days. He had rescued damsels in distress, shot a bunch of bad guys, was damn near killed by a grizzly, became rich serendipitously, and had possibly discovered his soul mate. *It has been a hell of a week*, he thought.

Chapter Sixteen

JT and Annabelle rode into Point Stevens Pass a day later, exhausted, sweaty, dirty, and hungry. They pulled up at the cemetery and rested their tired horses.

The graveyard was filled with people and carriages, and buckboards lined the road. There was a small tent, and JT heard a preacher speaking with reverence about someone. JT nodded to Annabelle. "See the two caskets? This can't be good."

As the preacher concluded, Dawn looked up at the tired arrivals and gave a start. She reached out to Dr. DeWitt on her right and a weeping Emma on her left, then moved toward JT and Annabelle. JT sat quietly, not wanting to interrupt the service and too tired to dismount. Dawn looked up and quietly said, "Emily and Millie are dead. And they burned down Emma's boarding house."

"They tried to rob the bank again and burned down the boarding house as a distraction," chimed in DeWitt. "Emily died in the fire, and they shot Millie and the sheriff in the bank."

"Who did this?" JT growled.

"Jean and Cain," replied Dawn. JT looked at Annabelle and shook his head in amazement. They dismounted and moved to comfort the women.

The service was now breaking up. "How about we head to my office? I don't know about you folks, but I could use a drink," said DeWitt.

Dawn nodded in agreement. The three climbed into the doctor's carriage and moved toward his office, with JT and Annabelle following closely behind.

DeWitt retrieved a bottle of brandy and began filling everyone's glasses. He raised his glass in a toast. "To Emily and Millie, may they rest in peace."

They all drank solemnly. Annabelle took a small sip and hugged Emma, who was wiping a tear from her eye. "And here's to our beloved Emma. I know she will carry on."

"Hear, hear," DeWitt chimed in.

JT looked at Annabelle and nodded toward Emma. "Well, we need to get rooms in the hotel. We need to get cleaned up, grab a sandwich, and take a nap."

Annabelle picked up on JT's nod and gave Emma one more hug, saying quietly, "We'll get a room for you, too."

Emma looked at her with a gentle smile. "That would be wonderful. I have no place to go."

With an exhausted sigh, JT turned toward the door. "Why don't we all get together for a late supper?" he said.

DeWitt nodded sagely and took Dawn's arm. "That sounds like a plan. Shall we see you in the hotel restaurant, about seven o'clock?"

Cain dismounted in front of the Lakeview Saloon, noticing Huck and the Sandman's horses in front. He frowned at the third horse, a tall, sturdy Appaloosa. Cain knew whom it belonged to, and he was definitely not a buddy.

He made his way into the bar where his two buddies were drinking rotgut and trying to ignore the drunken pig farmer in the corner. "Hi, boys. Why the hell are you drinking that crap?" he asked. "Grab me a bottle of the good scotch," he told the bartender, holding up three fingers for glasses.

Huck looked at Cain and said, "Where have you been? We rode out to the cabin but you weren't around."

Cain eyed him suspiciously. "Well, and did you camp out there and eat my food?"

Sandman picked up his glass, now full of good whiskey. "Naw, we never even went in. I've seen your sister shoot and I want to stay on her good side!"

"Well, it's too late for that. She would rather shoot you than look at you. She says you don't have a good side to you." Cain pointed at the pig farmer. "Speaking of not having a good side…," he whispered to Huck.

"Yeah, he's been riding us pretty hard and he's as drunk as they come," Huck said quietly.

"Hey Rudy, how's it going over there?" Cain called out.

Rudy looked up and replied, "What's it to you, bank robber?"

"Oh, nothing. I just thought you would like some good whiskey instead of that rotgut you're swilling."

Rudy stood up from the table, grabbed the half-empty bottle, and threw it to the floor. "That would be mighty nice, Mr. Bank Robber," he said with a smirk.

Cain gestured to the bartender, who reached under the bar for another bottle and moved tentatively toward the drunken pig farmer.

Cain looked the farmer up and down. He put his weight at 320 pounds and was at least six and a half feet tall. He was balder than a cue ball and had no neck to speak of. His head looked like it simply sat on his massive shoulders. His muscular arms were bigger than Cain's thighs, with a layer of fat all around them. His clothes looked like they had never been washed, and reeked of pig shit. But it was his eyes that gave Cain a start; they were almost yellow and hazy. They squinted in a drunken stare as the bartender gingerly put the scotch on the table.

Rudy gave the unsuspecting bartender a solid backhand, knocking him across the room and into the bar. "You move as slow as my damn grandmother, and she's been dead for nigh twenty years," he growled.

He picked up the bottle, removed the stopper, brought it slowly to his mouth, and guzzled half of it. He wiped his mouth on his sleeve and nodded his thanks. "Now that's some mighty fine whiskey, MR. BANK ROBBER," he said with a nasty laugh, then proceeded to guzzle the rest. Putting the bottle gently, almost reverently on the table, he belched like a thunderclap. His eyes crossed and he fell over backward, splintering the chair he had been sitting on.

The bartender moved toward Rudy, standing over him and making sure he was out cold. He cocked his leg and began to kick him in the head.

"Hey!" shouted Cain, putting a bullet into the ceiling. "Don't do that; he'll think it was me. Shoot him if you want to but don't mess with that pretty head." He turned back toward the bar, laughing. "Let's get the hell out of here," he said to his drunken buddies.

Chapter Seventeen

JT got to the reserved table in the hotel ahead of time and asked for his waitress. "I'd like to pay for the dinner tonight, and I'd like you to keep the drinks and food coming," he said, as he handed her a $20 gold coin. "You take good care of us; these folks have been through hell and back."

The rest of the crew arrived and ordered food and drink. The meal was unusually quiet with no one wanting to relive the past few days. As coffee and dessert were served, DeWitt looked around the table, cleared his throat, and took a sip of brandy. "Well, I guess it's up to me to explain what happened here," he said quietly. "Ask questions as needed, but I think you need to hear all of this."

When DeWitt was done with his tale of burning, bank robbing, and murder, JT said, "Thank you, doctor, that was very complete. But just one question: are you sure it was Jean and Cain?"

"Oh yes," DeWitt replied. "At least three people saw Jean with the sheriff and Millie, and two more saw Cain with a kerosene can. We showed them the wanted poster and they all confirmed it was them. Also, Stevens has put up a $2,000 reward on both of them and the county's reward is now up to $2,500 following the sheriff's death.

"Well, it's not about the money, but I'm going after them and I think I know exactly where they are," JT said to the group.

The dinner participants began to excuse themselves and JT whispered to Emma, "I'd like to chat with you for a minute if you don't mind." He looked at Annabelle and said, "We are just going to be a moment." Annabelle gave Emma a brief hug and said, "I'll meet you back in the room."

"Let's take a walk," JT said quietly. "If you don't mind, I'd like to see your lot." Emma shrugged and led the way.

Standing in front of the remains of the boarding house, JT gestured at the rubble. "I know this isn't a good time for this, but I'm leaving for Lakeview in the morning. I know how you loved this place and I'd like to help you rebuild it."

Emma looked at JT with doe eyes and said, "Oh no, I can't let you do that, but thank you so much for the offer. It really means a lot to me, but you don't really even know me!"

"Oh, I know enough to consider you a friend. I've come into quite a bit of money lately and I'd like to do this for you. If you like, I could make it a loan and you could repay it gradually, but I'd be happy to make it a gift. I know everyone would support me on this," he said with a smile.

Emma knelt down and picked up a small piece of burned wood. She smelled it and offered it to JT, who sniffed it with a puzzled look on his face. "What does that smell like?" she asked quietly.

"Um, burned wood," JT said with a frown.

"Oh no, not at all. That's my future! You're a good egg, JT," she said, planting a kiss on his cheek.

JT laughed, "Yes, I've been told that before!"

After walking Emma back, JT stopped at the mayor's house and knocked gently on the door. The mayor, who owned a dress shop with his wife, was a nice man with a perpetual smile on his face who gave discounts to the local women. He was elected by a landslide because the wives in the town insisted on it when their husbands voted.

"Hello, JT, how are you doing?" he said as he opened the door. Terribly distressing, all this."

"I'm OK, mayor, as well as can be expected," JT replied. "Listen, I'm headed after the bank robbers and I hope I come back! But in case I don't, I wanted you to be aware that I've set up an account with the bank's new owners to help Emma rebuild."

"That is very generous of you," the mayor replied. "You're a good man, JT."

JT smiled. "Not a good egg?" he said with a chuckle.

The mayor looked at him and grinned. "You know, now that you mention it…!"

JT laughed out loud.

JT woke up before dawn, hoping not to encounter Annabelle. He slipped out of the hotel and hurried quickly to the livery. Buck was apparently still asleep, so he quickly saddled his horses, giving them a pat and an apple. His saddlebags were full and his weapons were cleaned and loaded as he swung his leg onto Pete.

"Well big guy, where the heck are you going at the crack of dawn?" a voice said behind him. JT hung his head and turned toward Annabelle. "Aren't you going to even say goodbye?" she asked, her voice catching.

JT swung out of the saddle, put his hands on her shoulders, and wiped away the lone tear on her face. "I'm sorry, I should have told you, but I..."

Annabelle touched his face gently. "Shush," she said. "I know, and I understand. You would worry about me and I would be a distraction. Besides, I need to look after Emma. She told me what you offered her last night, and I'm proud of you. You go catch those murderers and come back to me in one piece."

JT gave her a tender hug, then remounted and moved quickly out the livery door with Annabelle trailing on foot. He looked over his shoulder and nodded as she waved.

"Go with God," she whispered to herself.

The trip to back to Lakeview was uneventful. JT decided to head to the saloon first for a beer and some hot food. As he entered, he surveyed the bar with a hand on his Colt. There were a few cowhands seated at a table drinking beer and a very large fellow at a table in the corner with nearly a full bottle of rotgut in front of him. JT bellied up to the bar. "I thought I'd see you again," the barkeep said, smiling.

"You did, did you?" JT replied. He pointed at the beer spigot.

The barkeep wiped off the bar in front of JT, drew a beer, and placed it in front of him with a flourish. "Oh yeah, those two bank robbers came back with their tail between their legs. Rumor has it they killed a sheriff and screwed up the robbery," he said.

"Well, they also killed two friends of mine. Burned one to death," JT replied with a frown.

"Yeah, that sounds like Jean, she loves to burn shit. We are damn lucky she hasn't burned down the town."

"Have you seen them recently?"

The barkeep nodded. "Cain, mostly. There ain't much else to do but fish and drink in this little town! He should roll in here shortly. Not so sure about his sister. She surely loves that cabin; goes back there every damn time they rob a bank. I guess they are just stupid."

"Well, I'm glad they're back, 'cause they are going to pay for what they did."

The barkeep set another beer down in front of JT. "Well then, this one is on the house. I got rabbit stew and fresh bread in back if you want some."

JT nodded. "That would be mighty nice."

JT finished his meal as the bar began to fill up. He pulled his hat down over his eyes, slipped the hammer strap off his Colt, and deliberately kept his back to the batwing doors. He watched whoever entered the saloon in the large mirror behind the bar.

The barkeep was coming with another beer, but JT waved him off as Cain and two companions came through the doors. They made their way to the bar without noticing JT.

"Give me two of those dandy bottles of scotch, and give one to my friend Rudy," Cain said, so everyone could hear.

Rudy looked up and grunted. "Well, I guess you're good for something," he said, as he moved the bottle of rotgut aside. While the barkeep cautiously took the bottle over to the pig farmer, Cain opened the second bottle and poured drinks for his friends.

JT turned toward the outlaw, motioning the cowboys next to him to step away from the bar. "Good to see you, Cain, you murdering scum!" he exclaimed.

Cain looked down the bar. "What the hell are you talking about, mister?"

"Yeah, a damn murdering scum and a home burner to boot," JT replied.

"How did you know that?" Cain blurted out.

The bartender shook his head and held his palms up, smiling at JT and mouthing *Stupid*. JT smiled at him and nodded.

"Here's what you're going to do, sonny," JT said with a smirk. "You're going to drop those guns and come back with me to stand trial."

Cain looked at his two pals and chuckled. "Are you out of your mind, mister?"

JT stepped away from the bar. "Well then, sonny, you best go for your guns." Nodding at Cain's buddies, he growled, "You want in on this too?"

"Not us," they replied as they grabbed the bottle and moved to a table.

Cain glared at them. "Thanks a lot," he said.

"Hey, we'll drink with you but we sure as hell ain't getting shot for you," they replied.

"Well, I guess it's just you and me," JT stated.

Cain put his hands down next to his two Colts, looking into JT's eyes and hoping for fear. He was greatly disappointed as all he saw was determination and disgust.

"After you, sonny boy," JT whispered, as he dropped his left leg to make himself a smaller target.

"God damn you!" Cain exclaimed as he pulled his right Colt first, putting a hot smoking bullet into where JT's heart had been a second ago. As he started to level his second Colt, JT put lead and death in the form of a .45 caliber bullet into Cain's heart.

Both of Cain's guns dropped to the floor as he clutched at his crimson chest with a stunned look of surprise. "God damn you," he said, his last words as he collapsed to the floor.

JT looked at the bartender, who was covering Cain's buddies with his Greener, and nodded his thanks just as the big fellow in the corner table stood up. "Hey mister, that was my whiskey supply you just killed!" he growled.

JT noticed that the big fellow wasn't wearing a gun, so he proceeded to replace the spent cartridges in his Colt. "Well hell, I'll buy you a drink," JT replied. "What's your name?"

"My name is Rudy and I'm going to beat the life out of you."

As he finished his drink, he threw the glass at JT and moved quickly around the table. JT dodged the glass artfully as he slid his Colt back into his holster. This Rudy was huge, taller than JT with arms the size of Arizona. He had to be more than 300 pounds, and not all of it was fat.

"OK, have it your way!" JT exclaimed, snapping two quick jabs to the face of his new dancing partner. He quickly sidestepped to his left, shoving a table out of the way and motioning to the other patrons to do the same. Within seconds, the fighters had a small ring for their battle.

Rudy spun and looped his arm at JT's face, but JT easily dodged it and dug a shot into his kidney. "So, what do you do, Rudy?" he said, as he leaned forward and sniffed. "Let me guess; you're a pig farmer?"

Rudy didn't reply but lunged toward JT and clipped him on the shoulder with a numbing punch. "Ouch, you win!" exclaimed JT, moving in quickly and snapping three hard jabs to Rudy's porcine eyes. "Or maybe not," he laughed.

JT continued to circle and snap jabs with an occasional body shot. He moved too quickly for the pig farmer to catch up. Most of the numerous wild punches Rudy was throwing were not connecting.

"OK," JT continued, batting away another mis-aimed blow. "So, you're a pig farmer. Nothing wrong with that. Hell, I love bacon myself. But do you have to sleep with them?" he said, as he danced around Rudy and put two more walloping punches into his kidneys. "Man, you stink."

Rudy rushed unexpectedly and wrapped his monster arms around JT's back and neck, picking him up off the floor. "Yeah, how do I smell now?" he grunted, as he began to squeeze the life out of JT.

JT's arms were pinned and his feet were not touching the floor. He began to see stars as his breath left him. His recent wounds hurt with a vengeance and he felt the stitches snap one at a time. He grimaced, looking up into the round ugly face of his opponent. In a heartbeat, he reared back and head-butted the smelly farmer at the base of the nose.

Rudy was completely taken by surprise and grabbed his broken nose, now gushing with blood. He bent forward, shaking his head and spraying crimson snot onto the onlookers. He stood up, wiped his face, and pulled a boot knife. JT stepped back, sucking wind into his lungs with the stars receding a bit. Rudy lunged forward and swiped at JT's left arm, cutting the forearm deeply. He then spun around quicker than anticipated and sliced a shallow groove into JT's chest.

JT backed up quickly and slammed into the wall, stopping his progress. He grabbed a stray chair on his left and weakly tossed it at his opponent. Rudy easily dodged it, wiping off his bloody face with his soiled sleeve. "Now I'm going to kill you, mister," he yelled as he lunged forward.

JT deftly slipped off his hammer strap and almost casually drew his trusty Colt. "Not so fast," he snarled, fanning three shots into the startled farmer.

Rudy looked down at his bloody chest. He straightened up to his full height, brought his arm back, and flipped the knife around to throw. JT cocked his pistol, took careful aim, and shot his bloody opponent straight between the eyes.

He slid down the wall, holding his bleeding arm. "Didn't your mama tell you not to bring a knife to a gunfight?" he asked, closing his eyes.

The bartender motioned at Cain's former friends with his shotgun. "Help him up," he said.

They grabbed a chair and sat JT up at the nearest table. He slumped onto the tabletop and moaned, then briefly raised his head as the bartender came over and put his hand on JT's shoulder. "I've sent someone to fetch the doc. You hang in there," he said.

After the doctor was done and most of the bar's customers had left, the barkeep sat at JT's table with a fresh bottle of scotch and two glasses. JT finished his third glass of water at the doctor's orders and took a sip of whiskey, feeling his newly bandaged forearm.

"Well, I've never seen anyone take Rudy like that, even before you shot the SOB," the barkeep said with a smile. "But ain't nobody going to miss him, except maybe his hogs."

JT replied, "Yeah, he surprised me with the knife, and I hated to kill him, but he gave me no choice."

"So now what?"

"Well, I'm gonna strap Cain's carcass over his horse and see if I can't catch his sister."

"You rest up a bit first. We'll strap on the body and leave him in the livery for you 'til you get back."

JT slid a gold coin out of his pocket and handed it over.

"Naw," the barkeep said, pushing the coin back. "Cain paid in advance for three cases of that fine Scotch whiskey, so I've been paid in spades."

JT nodded. "Why would he pay in advance?"

"'Cause his darn sister would have taken his money!" the barkeep said, laughing.

JT rode up to the smoldering remains of the Lakeview cabin. He scratched his face and looked around. Not only was the cabin burned, but also the small barn and even the outhouse. He shook his head, thinking, *My God, she surely loves to burn shit,* then turned and headed back to town. Looking at the woods as he kicked Pete and Re-Pete into a gallop, he hoped Jean wasn't lining up a shot.

Chapter Eighteen

Emma and Annabelle were having a late breakfast and bonding over coffee. Annabelle had brought Emma up to speed on all that happened in the cave, sans the lovemaking. She even showed her the bag of diamonds.

Emma nodded at the diary sitting on the breakfast table. "OK, there is a mystery in the desk. You know you want to go back. So, what are we waiting for?" she grinned.

Annabelle's eyes lit up. "What a wonderful idea! I know the way, and there's no telling how soon JT is coming back."

The duo left the restaurant after leaving a generous tip, checked out of the hotel, and made their way to the livery. Annabelle decided not to take the buckboard, knowing that her horse Ready had already made the trip. She quickly negotiated for three sturdy horses with extra saddlebags and extra grain for all of them.

Next, they visited the general store, where they loaded up with supplies and more kerosene. The last stop was the gunsmith, where she purchased rifles and shotguns, one of them a sawed-off Greener.

"Oh my!" Emma exclaimed as the clerk rang the purchases up with a smile. "I thought this was an adventure, not a war."

Annabelle responded, "My father said it doesn't hurt to have an extra gun or two and NEVER run out of ammunition!"

She pointed at a new .50 caliber repeating Winchester on the wall behind the counter.

"These are brand new, just got a couple in," the clerk said as he handed it to her. "Good guns, but mighty expensive!"

Annabelle took out a stack of bills and plopped it on the counter. "We'll take one. We also want plenty of ammunition for all the guns. Get as much as you think we'll need, then double it," she said with an evil grin.

Looking at the pile of money, the clerk nodded and smiled. "Yes ma'am, anything you say. I'll throw in extra scabbards as well at no charge."

Annabelle smirked. "I bet you will."

The clerk helped put the extra scabbards evenly on the horses as Emma climbed up onto her saddle. She looked around at a small crowd, which included Dawn and the doctor. Annabelle tipped the clerk and slid up expertly into the saddle.

"Where are you going?" Dawn called out.

Annabelle laughed, nudging her horse into a trot. "We are off on an adventure!" she cried as she left the murmuring crowd behind.

The first day was uneventful and they made good time under a sunny blue sky. Emma was uncharacteristically quiet, but Annabelle knew when to leave her alone. She would speak when she was good and ready, and if all the guns were a problem, then so be it. That night, in a familiar campsite, they made quick work of horse and meal duties and spread out their bedrolls. Emma was cleaning her new Greener with a smile on her face and Annabelle was reading the diary. As darkness set in, Annabelle threw a few small logs on the fire.

"Should we take turns at watch?" Annabelle suggested.

"Yes, that's a good idea," Emma said, with a quick smile. "I'll go first. I've got a lot on my mind and I don't think I can sleep anyway."

"OK, but wake me at midnight."

Emma moved from the fire with her back to a hefty tree trunk, waiting for night vision and trying not to look into the fire. Her father taught her that trick years before he died of pneumonia, along with her beloved mother. *They were good parents,* she thought. They were God-fearing and industrious and gave Emma, their only child, an opportunity to learn whatever she wanted. Her mother taught her to cook and her father taught her to fish, hunt, and shoot.

She relished the memory of hunting ducks in the fall with him, when the air was crisp and it was just the two of them together. He always gave her the first shot, and when she missed he did not reprimand her. He simply said "Next time," with his ever-present smile.

Emma had almost nodded off when she heard a strange horse whinny. She sat straight up and called quietly to Annabelle, tossing a small rock at her. Annabelle looked up and Emma pointed outside the camp, then stood up and leveled her new Greener. Annabelle nodded, picking up her Winchester and disappearing into the dark forest. Emma stepped behind the thick tree just as rifle shots peppered their bedrolls and fire. She waited patiently as she saw three shadows creeping into their campsite.

"Drop your guns," said Annabelle's voice from the darkness.

The shadowy marauders turned in unison and fired at the voice. Emma stepped out from behind her tree and triggered one barrel of her shotgun. She moved a step over and unloaded the second barrel at another target, then ducked behind the tree to reload. Muzzle flashes from Annabelle lit up the night as the third marauder let out a yelp, then turned and ran. Emma heard retreating hoof-beats while keeping an eye on the sprawled figures in the camp.

"Are you OK?" Annabelle whispered from the darkness.

"Yes, you? I think they are gone," Emma said, as she moved back into camp, pointing the reloaded shotgun at the unmoving bodies.

Annabelle came out of the darkness and threw a few small logs on the fire. She smiled at Emma, then walked over to the first man and prodded him in the back, ready to blow his head off if necessary. She rolled him over with the rifle barrel, revealing a face that she had never seen before. His eyes were wide open in death and his throat and chest were riddled with shotgun pellets.

Emma moved to the other man, who had fallen on his back. His face was missing but for a bulbous nose.

Annabelle moved up beside her. "Well, my friend, nicely done. Thank God you were awake," she said.

Emma nodded and began to shake. She dropped her gun as she moved to the edge of the camp, bent over, and threw up her dinner.

"I don't blame you," Annabelle said with a shudder, looking out at the darkness. She picked up a canteen and handed it to Emma. "Why don't you get some rest? I'll stand guard."

Emma nodded, picked up her shotgun, pulled out a spare blanket, and lay down. Holding the gun close to her chest, she closed her eyes as tears flowed down her face.

JT rode into Point Stevens Pass with Cain's body strapped to Re-Pete, keeping a good distance to avoid the stench of decay. People stopped on the boardwalk to watch but turned away when the smell hit them. He rode up to the jail as the mayor and Lewis Stevens approached, holding their kerchiefs over their noses.

"Who do you have there?" the mayor called out.

"Cain Cantrell. His sister Jean got away," JT said with disgust.

"Damn," uttered Stevens. "Well, take him over to the undertakers and we will get your reward in the morning."

"You mind doing that? I'm going to take a bath, burn my clothes, eat a hot meal, get a drink, and sleep for twelve hours." He untied the corpse from Re-Pete and headed for the livery.

Lewis Stevens moved toward the dead outlaw. "Sure, it's the least I can do," he said.

JT waved over his shoulder, making no reply. "Let's get you some grain and an apple or two," he said to his four-footed friends. Pete shook his head and trotted toward the livery.

JT woke up in the morning, refreshed but stiff. Looking at the back of his neck in the hotel mirror, he vowed to get it re-stitched and made his way down to breakfast.

Halfway through breakfast, Dawn and DeWitt hurried through the door and sat down at his table. "Well, hello," JT said. "Please sit down and make yourselves comfortable."

The doctor ordered coffees and turned immediately to JT with a scowl. "I'm sorry about this, JT, but Emma and Annabelle left without warning."

JT set down his coffee cup and sat up straight. "What? Tell me about it," he said.

"Well, they were having breakfast and apparently got the urge to go on an adventure, as they put it. But that's not the worst part; they took gallons of kerosene and enough guns to start a war!"

Dawn leaned forward, saying "And we don't even know where they went!"

JT sat back in his chair, thinking, *Kerosene? Oh, I know where they went.*

As the waitress brought coffee, JT pointed to his chilling cup. "Could you warm this up again? And I think I'm going to need another breakfast. I have a long ride ahead of me."

Chapter Nineteen

Annabelle nudged a sleepy Emma at dawn. "We need to get rolling as soon as possible," she said, as she handed her a cup of coffee.

Emma looked around, spotting the dead bodies on the ground. "Oh my, I hoped that was a nightmare. I guess it really did happen."

"Oh yes, "Annabelle replied. "So, let's get out of here before the others come back," she said, looking at the darkening sky. "Put on your slicker. We are going to get wet."

They headed for the cave with Annabelle leading the way. The rain stayed behind them until they were a mile from the mountainside cliffs and the cozy cave, then it came down so hard that neither rider could see a yard ahead. Annabelle whispered to Ready, "It's up to you, boy, go find our cave."

Ready looked over his shoulder and sped up. "Come on Emma," Annabelle shouted. "Follow us, we are almost there!"

She leaned down to hold onto her magnificent steed's neck, pulling her hat down and her slicker up. The rain seemed to intensify as they got to the narrow ledge leading to the cave. Ready paused at the start of the trail, but Annabelle gently kicked him in his flanks and he moved tentatively ahead on the treacherous trail. She called over her shoulder, "It's OK, Ready knows the way!"

JT supplied up at the mercantile store, then drifted over to the gunsmith's shop. "I wondered if you would stop in," said the clerk.

JT frowned. "Why's that?"

"Well, your girlfriend stopped in here and damn near bought me out!" he exclaimed. "Best damn day I've ever had."

"What did they buy?"

"Oh, I can't tell you that."

JT reached over the counter and grabbed the uncooperative jerk by the front of his shirt, pulling him half over the counter. "What did you say?" he hissed.

"Uh, lots of guns and ammo. Let me go and I'll go get you their receipt."

JT put him down with a thud and waited until he returned with the neatly itemized accounting. He looked it over quickly, then pocketed it and turned his steely glare on a cowering clerk.

"You doubled the price on the guns and tripled it on the ammunition, you low-life scum. If I had time, I'd beat the shit out of you," he growled, holding out his hand.

The clerk opened his till and quickly withdrew every dollar. JT's hand closed around the bills as he noticed an open box of expensive cigars on the counter. He closed the box and tucked it under his arm.

"OK, we will call it even, but if I were you I'd get out of town. The women aren't going to be so easy on you when they hear about this." JT waved the receipt. "They actually know how to use these guns!"

Mounting up after sticking the cigars in Re-Pete's saddlebags, he turned toward the trail that led to the cave. He waved at Dawn and DeWitt, who were standing in front of the hotel diner. His put his horses into a gallop and headed out on his own adventure, with an unlit cigar in his mouth and a frown on his face.

Annabelle entered the cave with the horses in tow. Sliding off her saddle, she helped Emma off her horse and out of her drenched slicker, then knelt down to light the pre-laid fire.

"My gosh, this is something," Emma said as she looked around the cave entrance.

"You haven't seen anything yet," Annabelle replied. Lighting a lantern, she motioned toward the fire.

"Sit here. I'm going to take the horses down to the end of the cave, but I'll be back in a bit." She put the saddlebags on the floor and set the kerosene away from the fire.

As she moved along the passage, she noted the wonderful condition the furniture was in, thinking, *Could go a long way in replacing the boarding house furniture.* At the cave's end, she stripped the horses, watered, and fed them. She sneaked

Ready an apple for guiding them to the cave and headed back to the entrance.

Emma had changed out of her wet clothes and discovered the coffee pot. She had built quite a large fire. Annabelle didn't comment, but quickly changed into something dry and sat next to the roaring fire, accepting a cup of coffee.

"Wow, this is something," Emma said. "Look at that armoire!"

Annabelle got up and opened the bottom door, pulling out the bottle of cognac. "JT thinks this is his, but the heck with him," she said with a smile, pouring a bit into each of their coffee cups. "Here's to our adventure," she toasted.

Emma frowned. "What's the matter?" Annabelle inquired.

"Well, I didn't think I'd have to kill someone, no less two. I've never killed anyone!" she lamented.

Annabelle nodded. "I know it's a life-changing event; I have killed a man before as well. But it was them or us, and you made the right decision. Now it's water under the bridge. So, what would you like to do next?"

Still frowning, Emma replied, "I'd like to go back and get started rebuilding my house."

"All right, whatever you like. We can go back tomorrow if the rain lets up, but in the meantime, I would like to examine that desk again."

Emma perked up. "Well, no time like the present," she said with a smile.

JT settled into in the now-familiar campsite as raindrops started to fall. He quickly put up a lean-to, took care of the horses, and had just started to build a fire away from the wind when the heavens opened with torrential rain. He sat under the meager shelter, made a pot of coffee, and chewed on some jerky.

He knew why Annabelle had gone on her adventure. She was a doer and needed someone to take care of. She was, after all, a nurse. Evil murderers had burned Emily and he knew she felt responsible for bringing her along. It didn't matter that there was no way she could have prevented what had happened. *Not logical,* he thought, *but so Annabelle.*

As the rain increased, he thought about having a nip of brandy and a cigar, but he hated to drink alone and it could be a long day tomorrow. So he wrapped himself in his bedroll and fitfully fell asleep.

Annabelle and Emma filled all the lanterns with kerosene and made their way toward the desk, with Annabelle stopping to explain the makeshift plumbing. Emma laughed at the innovation of the commode and vowed to use it when nature called. She stuck her hand in the ice-cold tub. "Not a chance of me taking a bath in that!" she said, with a wide smile on her face.

They gingerly moved the desk into the middle of the passage and surrounded it with lanterns turned up to the maximum. Emma sat down on the desk chair as Annabelle meticulously went over the desk inch by inch. After thirty fruitless minutes, she handed the lantern to Emma.

"Wait a minute!" Emma exclaimed, holding up the lantern to the legs of the chair. "Well, look at this," she said, as she removed a long rod with an end shaped like a key, and then another identical one.

"Hiding in plain sight," Annabelle murmured.

The keys were long rods over twenty inches long. They were made of copper and the ends looked like silver. They were round, not square, and not at all flexible.

"Hmm," Annabelle said, sitting down almost underneath the desk and holding up the lantern. "I'll be darned. Hand me a key."

She took it and gently inserted it into a tiny round hole, sliding it to the end. Emma looked at Annabelle and frowned. "Nothing happened," she said.

"Give me the other one, please," Annabelle replied. She slid it gently into an identical hole on the other side of the wide, shallow desk drawer, holding her breath.

As soon as the copper rod was snugly in the desk, a one-inch piece under the lip of the top of the desk popped open with no sound. Emma leaned down to discover a drawer with a knob that looked like a large ruby. "Open it," Annabelle said in a whisper.

Emma looked at Annabelle. "Oh no, this is your mystery desk. I'm just along for the ride. You open it."

JT awoke at dawn with an ache in his shoulders and neck and a throbbing pain in his wounded forearm, basically hurting all over. He looked out from under the lean-to, delighted to see that the rain had stopped. Stepping out of the makeshift shelter, he stretched and re-lit the fire. He did his morning duty and took care of his horses, talking to them individually as if they were human. Pete and Re-Pete pawed the ground as if they understood; the new packhorses didn't seem to have a clue. *Well, the Petes are special,* JT thought, as he gave them each an apple.

He took the time to cook a good breakfast, including the three unbroken eggs from his saddlebags. He loved eggs and could cook up any style, as long as they weren't poached. He could never get the hang of poaching an egg.

After breakfast, he cleaned, took down the lean-to and stowed it on a packhorse. He saddled up and headed for the cozy cave at a canter. *Cozy would be nice after this cold rain,* he thought with a grimace. He estimated he would get to the cave about noon, God and Indians willing.

151

Annabelle took a deep breath and pulled on the ruby knob. The dainty drawer slid effortlessly into her hands as if it were made to do so. She brought it down to the desktop, stepping back so Emma could take a peek. The top of the drawer was covered in purple velvet. "Go ahead, Annabelle," Emma said in the faintest whisper.

Annabelle slowly turned back the covering until it was completely removed. "Look at that!" she exclaimed joyfully.

"That is the most beautiful necklace I have ever seen," Emma said quietly. "I've never seen a diamond that big. And look at those emeralds; they are huge!" She counted six glistening emeralds all arranged around the huge diamond.

Annabelle leaned forward. "The rubies are bigger than the drawer's knob and are surrounded by diamonds too. These were made to be crown jewels," she said with reverence. "No wonder these people needed to flee the country!"

Lifting up the next layer of velvet, she exclaimed, "And look at all these loose gems! It's like a rainbow of color! I see diamond, ruby, sapphire, garnet, topaz, amethyst, opal, jade, moonstone…"

"How much do you think this is worth?" Emma whispered.

"I have no idea. Millions, I'm guessing, many millions." She covered the gems back up. Picking up the necklace, she put it under her arm.

Emma nodded and looked at the rest of the furniture. "Should we search all of them?"

"Heck no, let's get the hell out of here. I don't know why, but I'm feeling very vulnerable." Annabelle hurried toward the cave entrance, not even bothering to turn off the lanterns.

Emma looked around her. "Maybe we didn't bring enough guns," she whispered.

Chapter Twenty

Annabelle and Emma carefully wrapped their find, rolling up a towel to pad it and putting it in the bottom of Annabelle's saddlebag. They retrieved the horses from the end of the cave, extinguishing the lanterns behind them. Packing everything quickly, they saddled up and moved down the narrow path. There wasn't a cloud in the sky and the sun warmed them after being in the cold cave.

They rode side by side quietly, stunned by what they had discovered. The ground was nearly dry now and Annabelle thought they could make good time. They stopped briefly for an early lunch of water and beef jerky at a small stream, watering their horses before moving on.

Back on the trail, Annabelle took out her Winchester and surveyed the area with a grim look on her face.

"What is it?" Emma inquired.

Annabelle shook her head. "Don't know. Maybe nothing, but I got a bad feeling in my gut." Emma checked the Winchester on one side of her horse and the cut-down Greener on the other side.

Twenty minutes later, Annabelle pointed to the top of a small hill on their left, about 350 yards away. "We have company," she said, stopping her horse.

"Damn," Emma muttered under her breath.

Annabelle replaced her Winchester with the .50 caliber repeater and held her gaze on the stranger. He was too far away to see clearly, but he didn't seem to be holding a weapon. Annabelle thought she saw a flash of sunlight on his face and realized that he was watching them through a spyglass. "God damn it," she said, raising her .50 caliber.

"What are you doing?" Emma exclaimed.

"I'm not letting that stranger shoot first; I'm done with that crap. I'm going to scare him a bit and maybe he will go away."

Annabelle raised the Winchester, realizing it was the first time she had ever shot it, and aimed just below the stranger and his four horses. She triggered off three shots and the booms caused Emma to put her hands over her ears with a look of dismay on her face. Annabelle watched the stranger dive for the ground as one of his horses went down in a heap.

"Oh, damn!" she exclaimed. She saw Emma moving her lips. "What did you say?" Annabelle asked, realizing the three .50 caliber shots had deafened both of them.

No one moved. The stranger was prone on top of the hill. Remarkably, his horses had not bolted and one of them was sniffing at the dead horse.

Emma reached over and whacked Annabelle with her hat. She was pointing at the trail where three men were riding quickly toward them. Annabelle raised her .50 caliber and was about to shoot the nearest man when Emma reached over and grabbed the gun with surprising strength, shaking her head and frowning.

"What the hell?" Annabelle exclaimed as she reached over to their packhorse and pulled her shotgun out of its scabbard. She opened it, making sure it was loaded. Pulling out her short-range Winchester, she poked Emma in the side. "Take it, damn it," she insisted.

Emma paused, saying nothing, then reluctantly took the weapon as if it were red hot. As the three men pulled up in front of them, Annabelle said angrily, "You take the one on the right if we need to shoot, and don't hesitate!"

"Well, hello darlin's," the man on the left said. "We heard some shootin' and thought we'd lend a hand."

Annabelle pointed her cut-down at him. "Nope, don't need no help." She was trying to keep an eye on the man on the hilltop. Looking closely at the man with a sling on his right arm, she said, "How did you get hurt, stranger?"

He looked at his arm. "Ran into a door, nothing for you to worry about. I still got a good arm that can put a pretty lady like you to work, if you know what I mean," he said with a smirk. The other two were laughing and Emma looked like she wanted to hide under her horse.

Leaning forward, Annabelle said, "A door? Funny, doors don't bleed." Looking at his bulbous nose, she asked, "What's your brother's name?"

The stranger was taken aback by the sudden shift in the conversation and blurted out, "Frank. What's it to you?"

Annabelle said, "Well, I'm thinking we killed him last night. Couldn't miss that nose of his; he must have been as ugly as you," as she raised the cut-off Greener and pointed it at him. "So, what were you idiots doing sneaking into our camp in the middle of the night like cowards?"

The man looked at his riding partners. "That weren't us, and did you just call me a coward?"

"If the shoe fits…," Annabelle said, as she blew him out of the saddle. She quickly turned to the hombre next to him as he began to level his Colt. Aiming high and trying not to hit his horse, she took careful aim and blew his head clean off his shoulders. The horse didn't move. The body stayed upright for what seemed like an eternity, and then slumped over.

Annabelle looked over at Emma, hoping she would do her part, but was dismayed to see that Emma had dropped the Winchester and was sobbing.

The last man aimed his Colt at Annabelle, laughing. "I'm gonna shoot you full of holes, little lady, and then I'm going to enjoy your partner for a few days. And because you called us cowards, I'm gonna skin her in your memory."

He began to cock the gun. Annabelle closed her eyes and whispered to Jesus, knowing she had no more shells in her shotgun and her time on Earth was over. She heard a shot and flinched.

A moment passed and she opened her eyes. The man had been shot through the chest. His horse took off with the new corpse, which was bouncing off the rocky ground with a leg stuck in a stirrup.

JT stood on top of the hill, ready to take another shot with his own .50 caliber. He waved and yelled at the women. "Hello, you gals OK?"

Annabelle and Emma turned toward the voice, stunned. They didn't answer. "Hey it's me, JT," he shouted loudly.

Emma looked at Annabelle., her eyes wide. "What did he say? I can't hear a thing."

"It's JT. I think he said he's tired of rescuing me," Annabelle laughed.

JT stripped the saddlebags off his dead packhorse and gathered his horses, leading them down the gentle slope. He watched the two women slide off their saddles to disappear from view. Heading in their direction, he avoided the headless man who was still upright on his horse, which stood as if frozen. As he rounded behind the women's horses he stopped for a moment, watching Emma and Annabelle hug. They turned to JT.

"Hello, fancy meeting you here," he said with a chuckle. Annabelle looked at Emma and they both began to laugh, slowly at first. Eventually, they were holding their stomachs, rolling on the ground and almost crying.

Annabelle stood up first, finally getting herself under control. "Fancy," she said and started to laugh again.

JT smiled. *Stress and relief,* he thought.

He waited for the adrenaline and laughter to subside, then slid off his saddle and led the dead man's horse away from the group, pulling the corpse out of the saddle. He was about to pull off the saddle when he noticed what a fine animal he was. He led him over to the other horses and hung the saddlebags from his dead horse on him.

"Welcome to the family," he said, as he took an apple out of the bag and fed it to him. The horse made quick work of the tasty treat and nuzzled JT, then stomped his right leg. "Well, you're welcome," JT said with a chuckle.

He turned back the women, who were smiling and past their laughing jag. "Hello, big guy," Annabelle said. "You sure got here in the nick of time."

Actually, I got here too early," JT replied. "What's with shooting my packhorse?"

Annabelle hung her head. "I'm sorry about that, really I am."

"What were you shooting?"

"A brand new .50 caliber Winchester," she said with a grin.

"Well, it certainly did the job. You damn near killed us all!" he replied.

"I said I was sorry," Annabelle replied, a bit miffed.

"Hello, JT," said Emma, jumping into the conversation.

"Hello, Emma," JT said quietly. "How are you?"

"Better now that you're here. We have been to the cave and, JT, I think we solved the mystery," she said with a sparkle in her eye.

"Really? Do tell."

Annabelle stepped forward, looking at the surrounding hills and remembering the necklace in her saddlebag. "How about we curtail this discussion till we hit town?"

JT nodded as he looked around. "That's a good idea. Let's get out of here."

Chapter Twenty-One

The bedraggled trio rode up to the Point Stevens Pass hotel. JT said, "You two check in, and I'll take the horses to the livery. Why don't we get together for supper in a couple of hours?"

Annabelle nodded as she removed her saddlebags. "Sounds good, since the bank is closed," she replied. "We didn't get much sleep last night, so I'd like a nap."

As they made their way up the steps to the hotel, JT turned toward the livery with his small herd of horses, thinking, *Since the bank is closed? What is that about?*

Leaving the livery, JT stopped at DeWitt's office and was greeted at the door by Dawn, who was moving some medicines. "So you found them!" she exclaimed.

"I did," he replied. "They are at the hotel resting up, but I thought I'd invite you to supper with us."

"That would be very nice," Dawn replied. "Dr. DeWitt too?"

"Of course! He wouldn't go anywhere without his favorite nurse, would he?"

Dawn blushed and nodded, at a loss for words. JT spun around, waving over his shoulder.

"See you at the hotel café at 7."

Annabelle and Emma arrived at the hotel café deliberately early. Annabelle brought her saddlebags and her cut-down shotgun, taking a table in a remote corner. She put the saddlebags out of sight under the table and laid the Greener across her lap.

Dawn and the doctor arrived, holding hands with smiles on their faces. "Oh, it's so good to see you!" Dawn exclaimed as she sat down next to Annabelle. Noticing the weapon in her lap, she gave a start. Annabelle shook her head and pressed her lips with her finger. Eyes as big as saucers, Dawn nodded.

JT arrived, barbered, bathed, and smelling of aftershave. With a grin, he said, "I hope you don't mind that I invited the good doctor and his new assistant to dinner."

Annabelle smiled. The waiter arrived and she told him, "We would like your best bottle of champagne. We have something to celebrate!"

"Well, I'm glad I got a shave and a bath," JT chuckled.

The waiter bowed and left as Annabelle put the shotgun on the table and replaced it with the saddlebags on her lap.

"Whoa, what's with the cut-down?" JT exclaimed, almost standing up.

Annabelle waved him back down. "When you see what we discovered in our cave you may need to go get your Sharps."

The waiter returned with the champagne. He showed the bottle to Annabelle for approval, briefly glancing at the shotgun and paying it no mind as if everyone who came into the fancy café was armed with a shotgun. Annabelle nodded and the waiter opened the champagne, letting the cork bounce off the ceiling. He quickly poured a bit into Annabelle's glass. She sipped it and nodded, and the waiter filled everyone's glasses, set the bottle on ice, and left.

"I'm going to tell you all a story about a cave, a beautiful desk with a secret compartment, and once again being rescued by my knight in shining armor," Annabelle said, nodding at a grinning JT. "Some of this you might know, and some will be new to you, but bear with me, it has a happy ending," she said with wide smile.

The doctor picked up the bottle and divided up the champagne into the remaining glasses, motioning to the waiter to get the table another bottle.

Annabelle smiled and began her story. "Once upon a time, there was a cave..."

"And now here we are, safe and sound with good friends, and the future looks bright!" Annabelle finished.

After surveying the café and moving her shotgun closer, she brought out the cigar box and the bag of gems. "Here, pass them around. Don't drop the bag or I'll have to shoot you," she said, chuckling.

When the treasures had made it around the table, Annabelle put them back snugly in the saddlebag. She handed JT the Greener, then pulled out the necklace and slowly unwrapped it. "Ta-da!" she said.

The table was quiet. Annabelle picked up the masterpiece. Emma had, of course, already seen it, as had JT on Annabelle's return. JT smiled and passed it to DeWitt, who held it out in front of him.

"I don't know what to say. It is by far the most beautiful thing I've ever seen. It must be worth a king's ransom, and then some!" he exclaimed, as he passed it to a mesmerized Dawn. She held it in her hand and then gently held it up to her neck.

"Well, thank you very much," she said. "And it's not even my birthday!" The table erupted in quiet laughter as Dawn passed it back to Annabelle.

JT put the Greener on the table and whispered, "Put it on, princess." Everyone at the table nodded their agreement. Annabelle smiled and put the jeweled necklace to her throat, turning toward Dawn for help with the clasp. She beamed with pride as the dinner group quietly clapped and smiled.

"You look wonderful!" Emma exclaimed. "It looks like it was made for you, Princess Annabelle!"

JT lifted his champagne glass and proclaimed, "To Princess Annabelle. May you reign forever!"

JT heard the knock and smiled, knowing who it was. He opened the door and Annabelle swept into the room with a bottle of champagne and a wide grin. She handed the bottle to JT, noticing her saddlebags on the bed.

"Thanks for looking after the treasure," she said, moving them to a nearby chair. She sat down on the edge of the bed and patted the spot next to her. "Now come here, big guy," she purred.

With the morning sunlight streaming through the window, Annabelle snuggled into JT. "Well, what are we going to do now?" she asked.

JT looked at her. "Oh, I don't know, what do you think?"

"Now that I'm rich I'd like to get divorced. Marcus has been holding a trump card. He told me that if we got divorced, he'd stop paying for Madeline's education and supporting her acting and singing. And he's just mean enough to do it. But now...," she said with a smile.

"You can support her."

"Exactly. Also, there are some very good auction houses in New York where we could sell the necklaces."

"You don't like them?" JT chuckled. "You looked good wearing them last night."

"Very funny. I miss my daughter and I'd like to spend time with her."

"Well, I've never been to New York. Will you look after me?"

Annabelle smiled. "Oh, you bet, big guy, you bet!"

JT made arrangements at the livery for their horses and Annabelle went shopping for clothes and suitcases. She sent JT to the tailor for a suit, saying he could get better ones in New York. She bought a nice dress for herself and had most of the diamonds sewed into the hem. After a final meal with their friends, they set off on a New York adventure.

Chapter Twenty-Two

Three weeks later, JT and Annabelle stepped off the train in New York. The new Pullman cars had been a lot more comfortable than the cramped stagecoach that took them to the depot in Colorado, but they were more than ready for a bath and a soft bed. They transferred their belongings to a waiting carriage, and Annabelle gave the driver directions to a small hotel.

"You're about to meet some very nice people," she told JT.

There was no bellman at the quaint hotel, so JT and the driver brought the luggage in. Annabelle walked up to the small reception desk and rang the bell since no one was behind the counter.

Eventually, a small, gray-haired lady emerged from the back, holding an armful of towels. She exclaimed, "Annabelle, I'm so glad you're here!" She dropped the towels on the counter and hurried to give her a hug.

Annabelle reciprocated but stepped back, as the elderly woman was crying. "Mrs. Cusack, no need for tears! I'm glad to see you as well. Where's Mr. Cusack? He has been manning this reception counter for forty years!"

"Oh, Annabelle, he passed away nearly a year ago," Mrs. Cusack said sadly.

"Oh no! I'm so sorry to hear that. And where is Luther and his smile?"

"I had to let him go," she said sadly. "The business has not been good at all since Stan's death."

Annabelle looked around and spotted dust and marks on the paint. "Well, don't worry. Things can always get better," she said, giving the small woman a hug.

Mrs. Cusack nodded. "Oh, heavens me, let's get you up to your rooms. I'll give Annabelle the honeymoon suite, and you sir, something very nice as well," she said.

"I'm sorry; this is my good friend John Thurgood Thomas," Annabelle said.

JT shook the woman's hand. "Nice to meet you, Mrs. Cusack. I'm sorry about your loss."

She nodded and started to pick up a suitcase. "Well thank you, Mr. Thomas," she said, nodding at Annabelle. "Any friend of Annabelle's is a friend of mine. And welcome to New York!"

JT took the suitcase from her. "Please, call me JT. I'll take these. If you'll get the keys, we will follow you."

"Oh, my goodness, the keys!" she said as she hurried behind the counter. JT looked at Annabelle and shrugged his shoulders. Annabelle frowned back and grabbed another suitcase.

As they made their way to the beautiful, wide staircase, they passed a small but elegant bar that was currently closed. On the other side of the hallway was a small but intimate café, which was also dark. With towels in her arms, Mrs. Cusack explained, "I have an offer to buy the hotel from the owner of the Waldorf. He seems to be a nice man, but it's a very stingy offer."

They got to Annabelle's room first, truly a magnificent suite. "This was my honeymoon suite," she said to JT.

"Oh, I didn't want to say anything," said Mrs. Cusack, nodding at JT.

"That's OK, he knows all about it," Annabelle replied. "We are here to win my freedom and to get Madeline!"

"That's wonderful! She will be so pleased. She stops by and helps me out when she can. What a good girl she is!"

JT took his key and suitcases to his nicely decorated room. He returned to Annabelle's just as Mrs. Cusack was leaving. "JT, I've asked Mrs. Cusack to join us for dinner as our guest," Annabelle said.

JT nodded. "Yes, of course! Where would you like to eat?" he asked.

"How about the Waldorf, Mrs. Cusack?" Annabelle asked with a grin.

"Yes, their food is very good now that they stole my chef Michel Pierre. And he can always get me a table without a reservation," Mrs. Cusack said, with a sparkle in her eye.

The dinner party arrived at the magnificent hotel. Annabelle was wearing the dress with the diamonds hidden in the hem and had stored the necklaces in the bottom of her purse. JT looked handsome in his new suit, and Mrs. Cusack was dressed to the nines, ready for a night out in New York.

Mrs. Cusack approached the maitre d' with a smile on her face. "Good evening, Madame. Do you have a reservation?" he inquired.

"No, we don't, but if you would please ask Michel Pierre to come out here for a moment I'm sure something can be worked out," she replied.

The man frowned. "Oh, I'm sorry, he is very busy. That would not be possible."

Smiling, JT stepped up, held out his hand to the man, and dropped a twenty-dollar gold coin into it, which quickly disappeared. "Well, perhaps he could spare a moment. Whom shall I say is asking?" the maitre d' said with a smile.

"Mrs. C," she replied, with her own charming smile.

Michel Pierre appeared, threw up his hands, and grabbed Mrs. C by both hands. "It is so good to see you," he said, with a distinctive French accent. He stepped back. "And don't you look wonderful!"

He turned to the maitre d'. "Mrs. Cusack is my dearest friend, so please take good care of these people. Give them your best table!" he said. "Now I must run, but shall I order for all of you? Also, your first drink is on me!" he exclaimed.

"That would be wonderful," Mrs. C replied.

The maitre d' led them to a table at the side of the restaurant with a window view, picking the reserved sign discretely off the table. He bowed and snapped his fingers and a waiter appeared as if by magic. "This is William, and he will take good care of you," he said.

Mrs. C ordered a bottle of red wine after consulting with the wine steward. JT thought about the scotch back at Lakeview and ordered a glass with the help of the steward. "It is a 25-year-old single malt, and I'm sure you will enjoy it!" the man said with a flourish.

The waiter returned with the first course, a delightful shrimp stew, followed by a small serving of braised pork with pearl onions and grapes. Then came a salad with citrus and fennel, followed by duck à l'orange. The finale was roast leg of a lamb with honey and Dijon mustard, which JT had never tasted before. Dessert was crème brûlée with sweet liqueur flaming on top.

After coffee, Mrs. C turned to Annabelle. "So, I guess I didn't really need to get you each a room, did I?" she said with a brief laugh.

"Now why on earth would you say that?" Annabelle replied, looking at JT.

Mrs. C laughed harder. "Oh pshaw, I'm old but not blind." She turned her attention to JT. "You are a lucky man, JT, and I would tell you to take care of this wonderful woman but I suspect you already do that!"

JT smiled. "Oh yes indeed, I treat her like the princess she is."

"Good. When is the wedding?"

"Oh my gosh, Mrs. C, I'm not even divorced. And there is a generally a proposal involved," Annabelle said.

Mrs. C nodded. "No time like the present, Mr. Thomas!"

JT looked around. The restaurant was nearly empty. He knelt down, extracting a beautiful four-carat diamond from his pocket. He gently took Annabelle's hand and placed the stone in it.

"I think we can have a ring made to fit this," he said, blushing. "Annabelle Hewitt, will you marry me?"

"Oh yes, yes!" an ecstatic Annabelle exclaimed.

Mrs. C clapped quietly. "You were made for each other," she whispered. "May you live long and prosper."

JT woke next to Annabelle. There was a quiet rap at the door.

"It's me," Mrs. C called out. "There's coffee and fixings on a tray outside the door. I'm fixing breakfast just for you, so get up, you sleepyheads! And Annabelle, there's a special guest waiting for you downstairs," she exclaimed, as she retreated down the hall, singing and smiling.

Annabelle sat up at that. "A special guest? Oh my, do you think it's Madeline?"

JT retrieved the coffee tray. "It's possible," JT replied. "Let's get dressed and go see. I don't know why, but I'm starving!"

Annabelle smiled mischievously. "That's because you were up all night getting lots of exercise!"

The small café had a table set for four where Madeline was setting down a stack of pancakes next to the maple syrup. Madeline and Annabelle rushed together in a mother and daughter hug, tears running down their smiling faces. Mrs. C rose from her chair, dabbing her eyes with a handkerchief.

Annabelle introduced JT to Madeline, who asked him to call her Maddy. "Congratulations," she said warmly as they took their seats.

JT and Annabelle glanced up at Mrs. C, who spread her hands wide with a grin. "That's OK, she told me," Maddy said. "I'm so pleased for both of you. Maybe JT could be the father I never had."

JT looked across the table at a frowning Annabelle but did not respond. Filling the void, Mrs. C picked up a bowl of scrambled eggs and passed it to JT. She clapped her hands.

"Food is getting cold, people, and we can talk and eat at the same time. Try these; I think you will like them. They are made with something called cream cheese and the green flecks are chopped chives. Our good friend Bill Laurence invented this here in Chester, New York quite a few years ago. It's taken some time to catch on but you should try it on bagels. It really is magnificent."

They were all looking at her, smiling. Maddy started to giggle, followed by Annabelle, then a hearty laugh from JT. Mrs. C looked around the table, clutched her tummy, and joined in on the laughter.

The rest of the meal was spent with Annabelle and Maddy catching up on news of school, acting, singing, and local gossip. Annabelle made no mention of the cave and her newfound wealth until the dishes had been gathered and coffee was served.

"Well, we have some more good news," she said, putting her coffee cup down. She looked over at JT. "Do you want to tell it or should I?"

"Oh, you can, I'll chip in when needed," he replied.

"All right, this is a long story, so fill up your cups," she said with a smile on her face. This story is about a handsome rescuer, a cave full of beautiful furniture, bank robberies, losing good friends before their time and, finally, about riches beyond our wildest dreams."

Maddy and Mrs. C sat straight up in their chairs. As Annabelle got to the end of the story, she said, "Here's a sample," and withdrew the smaller necklace with the golden sleigh bells.

"My gosh, it is beautiful," Mrs. C said reverently.

"Yes, it is, isn't it?" Annabelle replied as she winked at JT. "But look at this!" She reached into her purse and gently extracted the Crown Jewels, as they had come to call the magnificent jeweled necklace.

Mrs. C stood up to get a closer look. "Oh my, oh my, oh my," she gasped.

Maddy looked at her mother with wonderment. "Can I touch it?" she asked in a whisper. Annabelle nodded. Maddy held the piece gently in her cupped hands. "It's so beautiful," she breathed, returning it to her mother.

Annabelle looked at Madeline. "This is what is going to set both of us free from your father. We'll have it appraised and then auction it off here in New York; there are some very reputable firms in the city. With the money from it and the other treasures, we will hire a very fine attorney and be done with him!" she stated firmly. Maddy nodded her agreement.

Mrs. C chimed in. "I know a fine lawyer who can help you with the other matter."

JT nodded. "Well then, we have a busy day ahead of us," he said. "To quote Mrs. Cusack: No time like the present!"

Mrs. C wrote a note introducing JT and Annabelle to the attorney and gave them directions to his office. She looked around and said, "Now, I have a hotel to run. Good luck!"

Annabelle hugged Maddy and sent her off to school, then repacked the treasures in her handbag. "Well, off we go on another adventure!" she said, smiling at JT.

JT chuckled and nodded. "Lead the way, princess."

Chapter Twenty-Three

The carriage pulled up to the four-story building that housed the law office of Spruce, Rubin, and Bernstein. Upon reaching the second floor, the receptionist greeted them warmly and took the note from Mrs. C. She looked up with a smile. "How is Mrs. Cusack?" she asked.

"Very well, but she dearly misses Stan," Annabelle responded.

"Yes, he was a wonderful man. Let me see if Mr. Bernstein is available. Please have a seat and I'll be right back." She passed through a door, taking the note with her.

She returned quickly, beckoning to JT and Annabelle. "He is just finishing up with someone. Please come with me and we will put you in the conference room. He should only be a minute or two. Would you like coffee?"

JT and Annabelle shook their heads.

They were just getting settled in the conference room when Morton Bernstein came charging in with a broad smile on his face. He was short of stature but somehow filled the room. His curly hair was turning gray and he had a paunch that he hid nicely with a superbly tailored suit and vest.

"Hello, hello," he said with a booming voice. "Allow me to introduce myself. Morton James Bernstein, at your service," he said with a smile. He nodded at the large table. "Please make yourselves comfortable." Turning to Annabelle, he asked, "How is the lovely Mrs. Cusack these days?"

"She is fine, thank you for asking. She has recommended you and your firm for a number of, what shall we call them?"

"Ah, projects," JT chimed in.

Bernstein nodded. "Wonderful. Projects is what we do," he said with a hearty laugh. "Tell me all about them."

When Annabelle finished her story, she looked up to find a dumbfounded attorney. Bernstein looked back and forth between the pair. He cleared his throat.

"I am speechless. Can you excuse me a moment? I would like to get my partners in here to hear this." He got up from the table and paused at the door. "Did you bring the, ah, jewels in question with you?"

Annabelle reached into her purse, gently withdrew the Crown Jewels, and placed them on the table with care. Bernstein tightened his grip on the doorknob. His face turned red and he steadied himself. "Oh my God," he said quietly. "I will be right back. Is there anything you need?"

"Well, if we need to tell the story again then perhaps some coffee, please," responded Annabelle.

"Coming right up!" Bernstein said as he left.

The receptionist returned with a tray of exquisite cups and a silver coffee carafe, cream, a bowl of sugar cubes, and delicate pastries. "I guess we are getting the royal treatment!" JT exclaimed, as he picked up a cup and handed it to Annabelle.

Annabelle smiled. "Well, I am a princess, after all," she laughed quietly.

Mr. Bernstein returned with his partners and brief introductions were made. "Please proceed," said the attorney.

After the story was retold, Annabelle sipped her cold cup of coffee as the lawyers looked at each other and nodded.

Mr. Bernstein spoke first. "First of all, we are prepared to represent you on this. We have no conflicts of interest. We certainly have heard of Marcus Payne, but have not represented him in the past.

"Frederick Spruce, on my right, specializes in real estate transactions. On my left is David Rubin. He is our generalist and he has much experience in divorce cases. I, on the other hand, am a criminal defense attorney, and while it seems that no crime has been committed, at least here in New York, I will orchestrate all that needs to happen."

JT looked at Annabelle and nodded. "We would very much like to retain you and your firm," Annabelle said as she emptied the sugar cube bowl onto the coffee tray. She then reached into her purse and retrieved the bag of diamonds, dumping them into the crystal bowl with a flourish. "Would you like a retainer to get started? Time is of the essence!"

Mr. Bernstein nodded at Mr. Spruce. "Frederick, why don't you talk about real estate and I will fetch Mike. I will have him bring a guard as well." Spruce nodded.

Bernstein explained, "Mike Goldsir is our resident jeweler. You may have passed by his establishment on the first floor.

We need to get all this appraised and secured as soon as possible," he stated firmly, and left the room.

Spruce turned to JT. "In regard to the cave, the furniture and the, ah, the jewels, we have a very defensible case. With the suicide note, the diary, and the fact that the original owners are deceased, you have a very strong case for keeping your incredible find," he said with a smile. "However, I think it is prudent to file a claim on the cozy cave, as you so delightfully described it, as well as the contents, as soon as we can."

JT sat up straight. "I didn't even think about that," he stammered. "Of course!"

"Well," Frederick chuckled, "you were a tad busy chasing robbers, shooting outlaws, and darn near being eaten by a bear!"

JT smiled and relaxed. "Well, when you describe it that way, I guess you're right!"

Annabelle patted JT's hand. "Don't forget about rescuing damsels in distress!" she said with a grin.

"Yes indeed," seconded Frederick. "But now we need to clean up, shall we say, loose ends."

"How do we go about doing that?" JT asked with a frown.

"Actually, we have just the man for the job. He is one of our investigators and a former federal marshal."

JT nodded. "Well, there are pieces of furniture in the cave that haven't been opened yet. Who knows what might be hiding in them?"

"Ah, not to worry. My man, Gregor Nelson is honest to a fault. I would stake my reputation on it. He is a recent widower and would jump at a chance to return to the west."

"All right, but I would like to meet him beforehand."

"By all means."

JT reached over and retrieved the bowl of sugarcoated diamonds. "I have one other issue regarding real estate, as long as we are on the subject," he said. "I'd like to buy Mrs. Cusack's hotel."

"Oh my, what a wonderful idea!" Annabelle exclaimed.

"Yes, and she can live there for as long as she wants!" JT said with a smile.

"And, and we could hire Michel Pierre back again and reopen the café, and, and...," Annabelle laughed and clapped her hands.

Frederick looked at both of them. "Well, it is very possible, as long as she agrees," he said, looking at the bowl of diamonds. "Good Lord, you could buy the Waldorf ten times over if you like!"

JT grinned. "One step at a time!"

A short time later, the door opened and Bernstein entered with a tall, narrow jeweler and two burly guards in uniform. Each guard had a gun in a shoulder holster and a shotgun in hand. They stepped to either side of the doorway and stood at attention. Goldsir stepped toward JT with his hand outstretched, but stopped mid-step when he spotted the jewels on the conference table. He stood nearly frozen.

"Well, well," Bernstein chuckled, "it seems Mike has found something to his liking."

The jeweler took the nearest unoccupied chair and reached over to the Crown Jewels, gently pulling them toward himself. He removed his jeweler's loupe without saying a word. He was careful not to touch the necklace but seemed to spend an eternity checking each stone, starting with the smallest and finishing with the largest. He picked up a small diamond, then a large one, and examined them.

Eventually, he remembered the others and extended his hand to JT. "Mike Goldsir," he said.

JT responded, "JT Thomas, and this is Annabelle Hewitt." Annabelle nodded from across the table.

"Pleased, in fact, very pleased to make your acquaintance," the jeweler replied. "Mr. Bernstein has filled me in on a bit of your story, and I've been assured that these magnificent pieces are not stolen, begging your pardon, and that you are in fact the clear owners. I would like to do a complete appraisal, but I can tell you now that these pieces are worth a king's ransom. Countries have gone to war over such pieces," he said, as the guards stood a little taller and gripped their shotguns even tighter.

Annabelle looked at JT and the color drained from her face as she slumped from her chair to the ground in a dead faint. JT rushed to her side while Bernstein opened the door and called for a glass of water. The receptionist rushed in, handing the water to JT. He sprinkled it on her face, lightly at first and then a bit heavier.

Annabelle's eyes opened. "What happened?" she asked.

"You fainted," replied JT.

Annabelle was seated after she assured the concerned attorneys that she was, in fact, OK. "Give me an estimate," she said emphatically.

Mike closed his eyes. "I will give you a very conservative answer because I haven't begun my work, but at the very least, four million dollars."

JT took a large drink of the water. "I think I'm going to faint too," he said with a laugh.

Mike stood, saying "I'd like to take these to my shop to finish my appraisal. You two are certainly welcome to join me and watch. If it were me, I wouldn't want these out of my sight for even a moment!"

"I have a better idea," said David Rubin, the only attorney who hadn't uttered a word. "Annabelle, you said time is of the essence, so perhaps Mr. Thomas might go with Mike to observe the appraisal while you and I discuss your pending matter with your husband."

"That's a splendid idea," Morton Bernstein chimed in.

Annabelle looked at JT, who spread his hands in an "it's up to you" gesture. She nodded at him and turned to David. "A very good idea. I would like to be free of Marcus as soon as humanly possible!"

Everyone returned to the conference room at the end of the day. JT spoke up first, nodding at Mike Goldsir. "First of all, I'd like to thank Mike for clearing the decks on short notice and for allowing me to look over his shoulder as he did the appraisal. As you see, we did not bring the find back with us. They are in Mike's vault, being guarded by his able security people. Regarding the valuations, I'd like to turn this over to Mike."

Mike stood up and cleared his throat, reading from prepared notes. "First of all, my hearty congratulations to the two of you. As to the valuations, the small necklace's appraised value is approximately fifty thousand dollars, the loose gems nearly a half million." He paused. "The Crown Jewels, as you have come to call them, have an appraised value of nearly four million dollars."

He looked at Annabelle, who smiled at him. "No, I'm not going to faint," she said, as she held up a full glass of water. Everyone in the room laughed.

"Mr. Thomas and Ms. Hewitt are committed to auctioning the magnificent necklace as soon as possible," Mike continued. "I would set the opening bid at five million and do it at a closed auction. I recommend Williams and Williams Auctioneers, where I know the principals very well. They can bring some of the wealthiest men and women of New York together on short notice for a find of this magnitude. I would be glad to help negotiate a reduced commission with the assistance of my friend Mr. Bernstein. As to the smaller necklace, the decision is yours whether to auction it or not. The diamonds I would separate, putting the five largest stones up for auction and keeping the rest in reserve, so to speak. They are very marketable and will rise in value over time."

Mike removed his glasses and glanced at the armed men. "Now, as for security, my guards will be on duty in my office all night. I have a cot and will stay as well. If you will meet me here at 9 a.m. tomorrow, we will, with your approval, move them into a vault at Chase National Bank. I must disclose that the president, John Thompson, is a friend of mine and I sit on the board. Will that do?"

Annabelle nodded and JT said, "Very good, Mr. Goldsir."

The jeweler smiled. "Excellent. I do apologize for being long-winded here, but this has been an extraordinary afternoon. And with that, I must take my leave. I have much to do." He bowed toward Annabelle and quickly left. Annabelle smiled and winked at JT, who smiled widely.

Rubin stood up and nodded at Annabelle. "Well, that is a tough act to follow," he said with a stern look on his face. The room exploded in laughter as he grinned mischievously.

"In all seriousness, we have made good progress. Annabelle, if you could spend the morning with me tomorrow while JT is at the bank, I think we can be prepared to serve Marcus the divorce papers by tomorrow afternoon. From what you have told me, I imagine it will serve to ruin his weekend," Rubin said with a grin.

Annabelle laughed out loud. "I will be here at 9 a.m. sharp."

Rubin nodded. "I will tell my clerk to draw up our contract for services immediately, and collect the required documents for the divorce."

"Please do. You know what is at stake on all fronts, so please do your very best work!"

"That I will."

Rubin turned to the others, "By the way, Annabelle has requested that I clarify a certain matter. Her married name is Payne, but she has chosen to use her maiden name Hewitt since the separation. We will, therefore, refer to her as Annabelle Hewitt in these proceedings," he said.

Everyone nodded to Annabelle. Spruce rose, looking at JT. "Perhaps after the bank, you and Annabelle would like to join Gregor Nelson for lunch. He is excited about a trip to Colorado and has some good ideas to run by you," he said. "We have some wonderful restaurants nearby and I'm sure you would enjoy them."

"That would be delightful," replied Annabelle. "I would like to meet Mr. Nelson as well."

Morton Bernstein rose. "Well, very good. This has been a most enlightening and, I dare say, prosperous day for all of us. If I had a glass of champagne, I would toast you," he smiled. "Perhaps at lunch tomorrow. We have a carriage waiting downstairs to take you back to Mrs. Cusack's hotel. Enjoy your evening, and we will see you tomorrow morning!"

Chapter Twenty-Four

As their carriage pulled up to the hotel, Mrs. C was standing at the top of the stairs. "My, my, quite a long day for you!" she exclaimed.

Annabelle gave her a hug. "Yes, it was a wonderful day, and thank you for recommending those attorneys. They certainly fit the bill."

JT squeezed Mrs. C's shoulder gently. "We have much to report and would like to take you to dinner again tonight," he said, as Annabelle nodded.

"Oh, that won't be necessary," she replied, and quickly turned into the hotel.

The newly-rich couple stepped through the doors and Annabelle stopped. "What smells so good?" she exclaimed.

"Oh, Michel Pierre is cooking for us, and I have been helping him," Mrs. C said proudly. "He must have bought out the market, and has a wonderful dinner planned for us!"

As they made their way into the café, Michel Pierre stuck his head out of the kitchen. "Welcome back," he said with a smile. "Mrs. C, I need you, pronto."

Turning to JT and Annabelle, he said, "I look forward to getting to know both of you. Mrs. C has told me the good news about your pending marriage, and we shall celebrate! You have an hour to refresh yourselves before dinner. No need to fuss, dress is casual," he winked.

Annabelle and JT arrived at the table as Mrs. C brought out a bottle of red wine. "This is from our wine cellar," she said proudly, displaying the label. She opened the bottle, sniffed the cork, and poured herself a bit. Taking a small sip, she declared it excellent and filled all of their glasses. "Hold on, I will retrieve Michel Pierre," she said.

As they returned, Michel Pierre took a glass from the table. He held it up and toasted, "To love!"

He drained the glass and said, "The dinner is almost ready. I have made it family style, so I will join you soon, and then we can get acquainted."

As Michel Pierre returned to the kitchen, Mrs. C leaned forward. "Now tell me all that happened!" she exclaimed.

JT looked at Annabelle with a nod. Annabelle started, "First of all, Mr. Bernstein sends his best wishes to you. He met with us initially, then…"

Mrs. C sat with rapt attention as Annabelle recounted the day, leaving out the part about potentially buying her hotel.

After Annabelle was finished, JT stood up. "Where could we get more of this delightful wine?"

"I have it right here," said Michel Pierre, returning from the kitchen to join the festivities. "I couldn't help hearing the last part about the Crown Jewels. Further congratulations are in order!" he said as he opened the bottle, refreshed their glasses, and sat down.

189

JT leaned forward. "Annabelle and I have a proposal, actually for both of you. We would like to buy your hotel for whatever you want to sell it to us for, Mrs. C, and we would like you, Michel Pierre, to come back as well. I'm not sure what they are paying you at the Waldorf, but if you agree to also assist Mrs. C in running this beautiful hotel, I assure you we will make it worth your while, and then some."

Annabelle jumped in. "We would also like to rehire anyone from the old staff who would like to return. Mrs. C, you may keep your suite for as long as you like, and help out only as needed, or not at all."

Michel Pierre, who had a wide grin on his face, nodded affirmatively at Mrs. C.

"Oh my," Mrs. C said, pouring herself another glass of wine and taking a hefty swallow. "This is the most wonderful news! I just can't believe it. I had been fretting about where I was going to live, and now…," she said with her eyes aglow and a tear running down her cheek. "Yes, I accept, yes, yes, yes!"

Michel Pierre stood up. "I do as well!"

They all touched their glasses together and smiled. Annabelle said, "That's wonderful. Perhaps we could drink some more of this wonderful wine and begin to work out the details?"

JT leaned forward, covering his glass. "The wine was very good, but if you don't mind, I'd like something a bit stronger," he said, looking at the array of whiskey behind the bar.

"What an excellent idea," Michel Pierre seconded, as he quickly finished his wine. Mrs. C leaned forward. "Well, more for us!" she said, winking at Annabelle.

JT and Annabelle arrived at the law office at 9 a.m. sharp, albeit with a slight hangover. JT accompanied Bernstein, two armed guards, and a sleepy Mike Goldsir to their appointment at the bank. Rubin escorted Annabelle to his office, all with the understanding that they would meet Frederick Spruce and Gregor Nelson for lunch at Keen's Chophouse.

JT and Bernstein arrived to find Frederick Spruce and Gregor Nelson already seated in the famous restaurant. Annabelle and Rubin soon arrived, and Bernstein introduced Gregor to the couple.

Once lunch was ordered, Bernstein gave a summary of their morning. He smiled at Annabelle. "Your jewels are locked in the vault and are safe, no pun intended," he chuckled. "The next step is to engage the auction house, and I have set up a meeting on Monday afternoon at our office. Is that convenient for both of you?"

"That would be fine," Annabelle confirmed with a brief smile, as JT nodded.

David Rubin leaned forward. "I'm delighted to report that Annabelle's husband will be served divorce papers after this meeting is done," he said, nodding and smiling at Gregor Nelson. "We will await his response but I anticipate his acquiescence since we are not asking him for one single dime. You have all met our chief investigator, Mr. Nelson. He will be serving the papers today. I'm afraid I will be without his assistance after this, as he is committed and, I dare say, excited about a Colorado adventure," he said with a chuckle.

Gregor sat up straight in his chair and gestured at JT. "I understand you wanted to meet me before you agreed to the trip. I think that is wise and I'm delighted to have met you both. I'm happy to answer any questions you may have. I am beyond excited for the opportunity. My late wife caused me to settle in New York and, truth be told, I would welcome a change of scenery, for at least a little while."

JT replied, "I know Frederick has explained this to you, but I'm concerned that we have unopened furniture in the cave that could be worth a small fortune."

Gregor nodded. "I completely understand. All I can say is that I have never stolen a thing in my life, and don't plan on starting now. I hate thieves. I have been a federal marshal, and have captured and caught thieves of all stripes, including horse thieves, bank robbers, jewelry thieves, train robbers, and burglars. Anyway, my dear departed wife would roll over in her grave and haunt me until the end of time. She left me all the money I will need for a lifetime, God rest her soul."

JT looked at Annabelle, who gave a nod of approval. "Well, Mr. Nelson, all I can say is welcome aboard!" JT exclaimed as he reached out to shake Gregor's hand.

"I have some ideas I would like to bounce off you if you don't mind," Gregor said.

"Not at all," replied JT.

"Well, I would like to file the claim on your cave as soon as possible. As I understand, it is off the beaten path, so to speak, but accessible."

"Yes, that's correct. For all I know, the cave is being looted as we speak."

"All the more reason to move quickly. Is there a person you trust in Point Stevens Pass who can help me pick out some quality help?"

Annabelle responded, "Yes, Emma is the former owner of the boarding house that burned down. I will write her a note of introduction. She has a vested interest in that she can claim the furniture in the cave, sans any valuables you recover. She doesn't know this yet, so I will tell her in my letter of introduction," she said, smiling at JT.

"I understand it may have been a mine before it became a furniture storehouse," Gregor said.

JT nodded. "Possibly, although we didn't really see any evidence of that."

"Well, with your permission, once your claim is filed I will engage an expert in such matters. Who knows, perhaps your furniture is hiding a gold or silver seam."

"Excellent idea. There are certainly qualified experts available there. We will leave the selection and hiring to you on this, along with any other matter regarding the mine."

Annabelle spoke up. "I am sure Emma will have some ideas for you. As you already know, she ran a thriving boarding house for many years and it wouldn't surprise me if a few of her former guests might fit the bill!"

"Excellent," Gregor responded, looking at the clock on the wall. "Now if you will all excuse me, I have papers to serve and a trip to prepare for."

Frederick Spruce leaned forward as Gregor left the restaurant. "Tell me what Mrs. C's reaction was to your proposal," he said eagerly.

Annabelle put her hands on the table and smiled. "She was thrilled, as are we. We are bringing back the former chef, Michel Pierre, in an expanded role. We worked out quite a few details over a bit too much wine, so no toast today, please! Now if we are through here, I'd like to head back to the hotel and take a nap!"

The next morning, JT and Annabelle woke up in an excellent mood and hurried down to breakfast. It was Saturday, and Madeline was going to join them.

They found her seated at the café table sporting a black eye. She jumped up and gave her mother a hug. "How are you?" Annabelle exclaimed.

"I'm OK," Maddy said with a frown.

"Maddy, what happened to your eye?"

"Oh, nothing. It can wait till after breakfast."

Annabelle looked at JT and subtly cocked her head toward the door.

"Um, I've already eaten. Anyway, I could use a long walk. I've been in too many meetings," he said and hurried out.

Annabelle turned to Madeline. "Tell me about the eye," she said quietly.

"Would you believe I ran into a door?" Maddy said with a grimace.

"No, I would not."

Maddy sighed. "My wonderful father hit me!"

"Oh my God!" Annabelle exclaimed.

"After grandma died, he started to drink. You know that, mother. Well, it's gotten worse, and when he gets drunk he blames me for you leaving. And then…," Maddy said, as she pointed to her eye.

"Are you telling me this has happened before?" Annabelle inquired with a scowl on her face. Maddy simply nodded.

"Well, you're not going back there. I'll get you a room here in the hotel," Annabelle said emphatically. "Then I'm going to kill him that bastard!!"

Annabelle and Mrs. C tucked Madeline into a room of her own. When JT returned, he was troubled by Annabelle's abbreviated version of the morning's discussions. "The question is, what do we do about it?" she asked.

JT looked at his future wife. "Can I make a suggestion?" he said.

"Yes, please."

"First of all, from what you said Maddy doesn't really want this known outside the family, at least at this point. And though Madeline is young, she has a good head on her shoulders. After all, she is your daughter."

Annabelle smiled. "Yes, that she is. And headstrong as well, just like me."

"Well, why don't you and Maddy disappear for a week or two? School is nearly over and she doesn't have any singing or acting projects on the horizon. It's a perfect opportunity for you to get reacquainted and lay out a plan for the future. It also keeps her out of harm's way for the meantime," he said.

Annabelle looked into JT's eyes. "What a wonderful idea! I know exactly where we can go in upstate New York. We can shop to our hearts' content and make up for lost time. If I can get her to open up about how long this has been going on with Marcus, it will help me win custody. Also, we can visit the Hudson River School of Art. I would love to get her enrolled there."

"Good. I'll stay here and work with the attorneys. There's an auction to plan, and I need to ride herd on Gregor Nelson until he gets situated in Point Stevens Pass. I also want to upgrade our new hotel and bring back any old staffers who are willing, along with any new ones we might need."

"You are going to be one busy man!"

JT grinned. "You can talk it over with Maddy after her nap, and then we can all go out to dinner tonight."

Annabelle looked into JT's eyes. "You are so wise. Did I ever tell you that you are a good egg?"

"Why, I believe so."

Maddy readily agreed to the plan, smiling widely when Annabelle talked about shopping for clothes and shoes. The next day was spent planning the trip while Maddy sneaked home for a few clothes, avoiding her father.

JT and Annabelle made the most of their last night together for a while, and morning came too quickly. Mrs. C had arranged for a carriage, which was already waiting to take mother and daughter to their train at Pennsylvania Station.

"Hurry, dears, don't be late! And come back soon!" she said, hugging them both.

JT was surprised when Maddy gave him a quick hug before the driver helped her up. He and Annabelle hugged a good bit longer and, with a kiss, the two were off.

JT put his arm around Mrs. C and gave her a gentle squeeze. "Well, we have a lot of work to do. Are you ready?" he asked.

"Absolutely," she said and looked at the disappearing carriage. "I think Maddy is going to be all right."

Chapter Twenty-Five

The next few weeks were a whirlwind of activity as the hotel was thoroughly cleaned, repainted and repaired. New linens were bought and quite a few mattresses were replaced, along with additional gas lights for the halls and rooms. Fresh flowers were readily apparent, the furniture gleamed, and even the reception bell had been replaced.

Michel Pierre supervised the revamp of the kitchen, thanking JT every day for giving him free rein. "My kitchen may never be as big as the Waldorf's, but it will be better in every way!" he beamed.

Mrs. C located Luther, the bellhop, and rehired him immediately. Michel's uncle Raphael was also brought on to run the reception desk. "He is a man of many talents, and will certainly keep unruly guests in check," Michel declared.

Five and a half weeks later, JT stood at the bottom of the stairs, waiting for Annabelle and Madeline to return from their adventure. He had gotten a wire giving him notice of their arrival two days beforehand and had hurried the workers to finish before they got home. He had much news to report, both good and bad, as he stood anxiously looking at the cloudy street.

Annabelle's engagement ring was in his pocket, a carved gold band holding a 4.85-carat diamond with smaller square-cut diamonds in the setting. JT didn't know much about jewelry, but when he held it up to the morning sunlight he was impressed with its beauty. Mike Goldsir had also been impressed; not everyone could afford such a ring.

"Oh, here they come," exclaimed Mrs. C, pointing down the street.

The carriage pulled up to the front of the hotel, followed by another carriage that pulled in behind them. A young man sitting next to the driver and holding a shotgun hopped down, nodded at JT, and helped Madeline and Annabelle out of the carriage. They were dressed to the hilt, each with a fashionable hat on their heads and a smile on their faces.

Annabelle rushed to JT and gave him a kiss and a prolonged hug. Maddy offered her hand and curtsied as the young man hovered next to her. Mrs. C hurried down the steps and joined the hug fest.

Annabelle looked at Luther, who was smiling his trademark smile. "Oh, so good to see you, Luther!" she exclaimed.

Luther nodded respectfully. "Very good to see you, ma'am. It's been a while."

"And who is this young man?"

"This is my grandson Luther Eli Earp. We call him Lee for short. Goes with his initials, you see."

"Nice to meet you, Lee."

Lee bowed. "The pleasure is mine, madam."

Annabelle looked over at Luther, who was beaming broadly. "Well, isn't he well mannered!" she said.

"Shall we take your things to your rooms?" Luther asked.

"Yes, please," Annabelle said as she pointed at the second carriage, which was filled with packages. "There's quite a lot. We got a bit carried away," she said with delight.

Annabelle took JT's arm as she mounted the steps, noticing the banner over the door that read "Welcome Home." Stepping inside, she drew in her breath. "My gosh, everything looks new!" she exclaimed.

"Well, we have been busy," JT commented as they made their way to the reception desk.

The clerk stood at attention, looking as if he were about to salute. Mrs. C scooted around the desk and touched him lightly on the elbow. "And this is Raphael. He is our new addition and will make sure you get everything you need!" she said, beaming.

"I'm at your service, ladies," Raphael said. "Please follow me. Your rooms have been redone, and we all hope that you will like them." He took the room keys and led the way up the staircase.

Annabelle commented about how fresh everything felt as she picked a rose out of a vase and held it to her nose. "Fresh flowers," she commented, looking at Mrs. C. "Whose idea was this?"

Mrs. C. laughed briefly. "Believe it or not, it was JT's."

Annabelle looked at JT as he blushed. "Well, aren't you full of surprises?"

JT looked straight ahead as they continued to climb the stairs. "Well, I like flowers, what's wrong with that?" he said with a slight frown.

"Not a thing, big guy, not a thing," she said as she hugged his elbow and sniffed the rose again.

As wonderful smells arose from Michel Pierre's busy kitchen, Raphael knocked discretely on Annabelle and JT's door. "Dinner is served," he called out, then left hurriedly.

JT gave Annabelle one last kiss and hurried to get dressed. Annabelle, still lounging on the bed, said, "I'll be down in ten minutes. You go down and entertain people. By the way, I invited Maddy's new friend Timothy to dinner."

"You mean the big guy with the shotgun? Why did you invite him?" JT replied.

"Yes, I guess he is big, but gentle as a lamb–unless he isn't!" she said with a smirk.

"What do you mean? Is he a danger to Maddy? I saw how he looked at her and followed her around like a puppy! Should I go have a talk with him?" JT asked, with a touch of anger.

Annabelle sat on the edge of the bed, sans clothes, and began to laugh. "Sit down, JT. They can wait for us downstairs. You need to hear this story."

"First of all, your idea of a trip was wonderful. It was exactly what Madeline needed. Me too, for that matter. We moved from town to town, shopping and eating, sleeping in when we wanted and more importantly just catching up and bonding like never before. I had always wanted to see Niagara Falls and Maddy thought it would be a fun adventure. Well, we did and the next day we were shopping for some souvenirs. It was the end of the day and we were loaded down with packages when two drunken locals accosted us on the sidewalk. They wanted…well, you know what they wanted, and were not about to take no for an answer."

"I was about to scream for help when Timothy came out of nowhere. He quietly slid up behind them, smashed their heads together, and removed their Colts from their holsters before they hit the ground! It happened so fast, and it was a sight to behold! He actually grabbed them by the collars and dumped them in the street."

"Since then he has been a self-appointed bodyguard to Maddy. We invited him to dinner and were surprised to learn he is an artist, or studying to be one. He is attending the Pratt Institute of Art here in New York. As soon as I heard that I hired him. He won't take any money, so we feed him!" Annabelle said with a laugh. "And he eats like a horse."

JT and Annabelle arrived at dinner a little late and found everyone already at the table. Maddy, of course, was sitting next to Timothy. JT was surprised to see Raphael seated next to Mrs. C, but made no comment.

As the men rose, to greet them, JT stopped next to Timothy and extended his hand. "Thank you for looking after our girls. I appreciate it, and perhaps we should chat tomorrow about a part-time job here at the hotel," he said.

"That would be wonderful, and you're welcome," Timothy replied.

Maddy smiled at JT and pulled Timothy back into his seat. "I'm starving," she said, patting her tummy just as the kitchen doors opened. Michel Pierre and his two helpers descended on the diners with plates piled high and aromas from out of this world. JT hurriedly sat down.

The dinner was the best JT had ever had in his life. They were served clam chowder, braised scallops, stuffed capons, medallions of veal, fresh-baked bread, salads, and a variety of desserts from an ornate rolling tray. JT noticed that Timothy, who hadn't spoken a word, was trying every dish with a smile of joy on his face.

The meal was nearly finished when Annabelle looked at Raphael. "I understand you are Michel Pierre's uncle," she said.

"Yes, yes I am," he replied.

"I thought I sensed a, how should I put it, a military bearing in you. Is that correct?"

"Oh yes. I was a lieutenant in the French army for sixteen years, then a captain for another eight years in the Foreign Legion," he said, unconsciously sitting straighter as he spoke. "After fighting in Mexico, I retired and came to your country to settle down, with the help of my nephew."

"Well, welcome to America and to our little family," Annabelle said. Turning to Mrs. C, she commented, "It is amazing what you have done with your hotel in such a short time."

JT cleared his throat. "Actually, it's now your hotel too. At least once you sign the papers."

"That's wonderful!" Annabelle exclaimed. "Now, tell me what else has been happening here while Madeline and I were buying every shoe in New York."

JT frowned. "Well, your husband stopped by one morning, and he was quite drunk."

"Oh, no!" Annabelle exclaimed.

"He had a two-bit sheriff with him and he was none too happy that you weren't here. Basically, he said there is no way he is allowing you to divorce him and he, will see you rot in hell first!"

Annabelle laughed, which surprised everyone at the table. "Yes, that sounds like Marcus. We will just see about that!"

Madeline leaned forward. "So, what did you do?" she asked.

JT looked at Raphael. "Why don't you answer that question?" he said with a smile.

Raphael nodded. "Well, we threw him out and told him never to come back."

"How in the world did you do that?" Annabelle asked.

Raphael quickly stood up from his chair. In the blink of an eye, he raised his right arm out straight and twisted his wrist. A two-shot derringer popped out and slid smoothly into his hand. The gun looked quite lethal despite its size. He showed it to everyone, then sat down with a smile on his face.

"It was a sight to see," grinned JT. He looked around and said, "I have an announcement to make. The auction will be held a week from today. The response has been overwhelming, simply based on a description of the necklace."

"That's wonderful," said Annabelle. "Wait until they see it up close!"

The week flew by as everyone pitched in to reopen the hotel. It was decided that JT and Annabelle would go to the auction along with Mr. Bernstein, and the rest of the group would stay behind to prepare a celebration in the hotel café.

JT wore a new pinstriped suit and Annabelle was dressed in a striped skirt with a matching long, fitted jacket. Its three-quarter sleeves were just the right length to show off her new bracelets. Around her neck was the "sleigh bell" necklace, which she and JT had decided to keep as a memento of their good fortune.

The carriage pulled up in front of the hotel with everyone there to see them off, including the staff. Annabelle waved as they pulled away. "What a wonderful group," she commented.

JT simply nodded and smiled.

Chapter Twenty-Six

The auction hall was filling up as Mr. Bernstein and the manager met JT and Annabelle at the door. They were led to their reserved seats in the front row of the small auditorium.

"This is so exciting!" Annabelle exclaimed. "Yes, it is," JT replied. "I'm told it could go quickly since we are only offering the five diamonds and the Crown Jewels."

Annabelle looked around. She reached out, took JT's forearm, and squeezed. "Oh my God, look at that," she said, facing the rear of the auditorium.

JT and Bernstein turned their heads. "What the hell is Marcus doing here?" JT exclaimed, starting to get up, but Bernstein grabbed him by the arm and pulled him back into his seat

"He is with Judge Cavanaugh and his wife, so I assume he is their guest," Bernstein said. "The wife is the wealthy one and the judge is the slippery one. He is known to solicit bribes, though he's never been caught. She has the money, but he loves the ladies and his whiskey a bit too much and she is not about to support that nonsense. Somehow, he always seems to have plenty of cash, though, and it's easy to guess how."

As Marcus noticed them looking at him, he nudged the man next to him. Both of them nodded and laughed.

"Now, who is that?" Annabelle inquired.

"Oh, that is Sheriff Duvall. He's even more slippery than the judge," Bernstein replied.

Annabelle turned around. "Well, let's ignore them. This is our night and they are not going to spoil it!"

"Hear, hear," Bernstein seconded.

JT was the last to turn around, with a frown on his face. "They are up to no good," he whispered to himself.

The manager stepped up to the podium, nodding at Annabelle and JT. At the rear of the hall, six well-armed men came through the doors, accompanied by the auctioneer, who held the Crown Jewels. The doors were quickly locked. The auctioneer put the necklace on a small table, and the guards took a position on either side.

Back at the podium, the manager read from his notes. "This afternoon we are delighted to offer an incredible piece, what we have come to call 'The Crown Jewels of the Cave.'" Annabelle gripped JT's arm and giggled.

He continued, "Given that none of you have seen this stunning necklace, we are going to do things a bit differently. We are going to have you walk by the jewels without touching them. Once everyone returns to their seats, we will begin the auction. The necklace has been appraised by one of New York's finest jewelers, Mike Goldsir. He is present in the room and can answer any questions for the lucky buyer."

Goldsir rose and tipped an imaginary cap before sitting back down.

"Prior to that, however, we are going to auction off five incredible diamonds that you have already had the opportunity to view. So without further ado, I'm delighted to introduce Williams and Williams' senior auctioneer, Sean Cubert."

The diamond auction went very quickly. Everything went to an anonymous bidder represented by a well-known attorney. JT and Annabelle could not have been more pleased, as they sold for well over the appraised value.

With the main event at hand, the participants murmured as the manager took over the podium.

"You will all be allowed to walk past the necklace," he said. "Please do not touch it. I repeat, do not touch it. If you do you will not be allowed to bid! Each row will go separately. Just imagine you're at church," he said, breaking the tension. "If you have never been to church just follow the person in front of you."

The crowd laughed as the guards moved forward to cover the first and second aisles, then the procession began. The potential bidders moved along until the last row was moving past the necklace.

Marcus Payne stopped, obviously drunk, and stooped to touch the necklace. Both guards quickly moved their shotguns, one to his neck and one to his stomach, as if they had practiced the move for hours. Marcus held his hands in the air, staring at the guards as he backed off and moved on.

Annabelle turned to JT. "I guess he's not going to bid," she said with a smirk.

Sean Cubert stepped up to the podium and banged a gavel to get everyone's attention. The starting bid is five million dollars," he said succinctly. "Do I have a starting bid?"

Mrs. Cavanaugh raised her hand slightly and said "Six million dollars."

A voice from the front declared "Seven million," followed immediately by "Seven million five," from the side. The judge's wife countered with "Eight million."

Marcus elbowed the sheriff in the side with a wide grin on his face. The attorney representing the anonymous bidder turned in his seat and looked across the auditorium at Mrs. Cavanaugh. He raised his hand and nodded at the auctioneer. "Ten million dollars," he said clearly.

The judge looked at his wife, grabbing her hands and shaking his head with a frown as the color drained from his face. She looked at him with disgust but said nothing.

Cubert called out, "I have ten million. Any other bids?" Everyone sat silently. "Going once at ten million dollars, going two times for ten million dollars." He paused.

"SOLD for ten million dollars," Cubert said as he banged his gavel sharply on the podium.

The crowd began to break up. As Annabelle and JT hugged, Mr. Bernstein shook JT's hand until JT needed to stop him and retrieve it with a laugh. A line of disappointed bidders formed, congratulating both of them until the auditorium was empty but for the three of them.

They made their way to the street, stepping outside as a clerk locked the door behind them and scooted away. "So, who was the mysterious bidder?" Annabelle asked Bernstein.

"Well, I have it on good sources that it is Mr. Rockefeller himself," he said, as he puffed out his chest.

"Oh my," gasped Annabelle. "Well, I guess he certainly could afford it!"

"Hmm, I wonder how he will look wearing it?" JT said with a chuckle.

Mr. Bernstein turned serious. "Actually, Mr. Rockefeller winning the auction is very good for us. As you know, the Crown Jewels came out of nowhere, so to speak, with no indication of ownership nor bill of sale. I mean no offense to you, of course. But now that Mr. Rockefeller has purchased the necklace, no one will question where it came from!"

He stepped up into his waiting one-horse brougham, looking around the empty street for JT and Annabelle's carriage. "Your driver appears to be late. Why don't I give you a lift back to your hotel?" he said.

JT looked at Annabelle. "It's your call," he said.

"Oh, he will be here in a minute. For what we have paid him in the last month, he'd better be!" she stated firmly.

JT shrugged. "We will be fine. The rain seems to have stopped. If he doesn't show up soon, it's a nice night for a walk anyway."

"All right," Bernstein said. "We will see you in our offices tomorrow to wrap this auction up and deposit your money," he said with a smile as his carriage pulled away.

JT and Annabelle waited nearly twenty minutes for the carriage. They tried the door to the auction house but it was locked. Annabelle looked down the empty street. "Come on JT, it's a nice night for a walk," she said, as she took his arm.

JT nodded, wishing he had brought a pistol with him. "Well, I guess we have no choice," he stated. "But first, let me give you this. I know it's a bit premature and Mike Goldsir said you need to come in and get the band adjusted, whatever that means!"

With that, he slipped the stunning engagement ring on her finger. "He also has a few wedding bands I looked at that you may like!"

Annabelle gasped as she held the ring out in front of her. "It is beautiful, just gorgeous!" she said, giving JT a kiss and a prolonged hug. "I love you JT, don't you ever leave me!" she exclaimed.

"I love you too," JT replied, "and I won't!" He took her arm and turned up the street. "People are waiting for us, so we best get back to the hotel."

The night was actually very nice, and they chatted about the auction and a potential wedding date. Annabelle thought she would like a large wedding and JT thought a smaller, more intimate ceremony would be best. Neither one noticed the lurking figure who stepped out of a darkened doorway.

JT heard a sound and tried to turn, but Annabelle was holding tightly to his arm and he felt the blow to the back of his head before he could pivot. He smelled whiskey as he slipped to the ground and started to lose consciousness.

Annabelle turned to face her assailant. "Marcus Payne, what have you done?" she exclaimed.

Marcus shuffled toward her, holding up a revolver in his right hand. "I told you I would never let you go," he said. Seeing the engagement ring on her finger., he growled, "Look at that. Already moved on, and not even divorced yet."

He paused, taking a wobbly step backward as he brought the gun up chest high, holding it in both hands.

Annabelle put her hands out in front of her. "You can't do this Marcus, you just can't!"

He pulled the trigger with his shaking hands. The muzzle exploded with fire, smoke, and Annabelle's death. The slug passed through her left palm and entered her chest above her heart.

Annabelle looked down at the spreading crimson stain. "Go to hell, Marcus Payne!" she exclaimed and crumpled to the ground, dead before she hit.

Marcus looked around at the empty street. He pulled JT over to the doorway and moved his head onto the brick edge of the building, making it look as if he had hit his head while falling backward. He put the revolver in JT's hand, took one more look around, and quickly left the scene.

Chapter Twenty-Seven

JT woke up with a splitting headache and fuzzy vision. The first thing he saw was a stained ceiling. He moved his head gingerly to the left and saw a wall, then to the right and saw bars where a wall should be. He sat up straight, ignoring the pounding in his head. *Bars? Am I in jail? What the hell am I doing in jail?*

He lay back down, relieving the pressure and trying to remember. *We had the auction. The carriage didn't show up, and we were walking back to the hotel.* It all came rushing back to him. He felt the back of his head. *Someone hit me on the head; someone smelling of booze.*

He sat up as the jailer appeared. "Why the hell am I in jail?" he demanded.

The jailer ignored the question. "You have a visitor," he said as he swung the door back. Morton Bernstein swept into the room. as the jailer retreated up the hall.

"What the hell happened and what am I doing in here?" JT shouted before his throbbing head got the best of him. "Why am I here?"

Bernstein leaned on the wall. "Don't you remember?" he asked.

"Well, I remember you leaving, and Annabelle and I walking. And I remember the smell of whiskey just before someone gave me this," JT said as he touched the egg on the back of his head.

Bernstein nodded." That makes sense," he said, more to himself. "I hate to be the one to tell you this, but..." He paused, looking away with a tear rolling down his face. "Annabelle is dead."

JT stood up and moved toward him. "What did you say? Annabelle is what?"

Bernstein took JT's arm and sat him down on the bed. "Annabelle is dead. Someone shot her through the heart."

"Oh no, that can't be, we were just planning our wedding, planning our future together."

"It gets worse, JT. They say you killed her!"

JT lay back down on the bed and covered his eyes, not saying a word. Finally, he sat back up. "Tell me all you know. I loved Annabelle. We were going to get married. I would never harm her!"

"I know," the attorney exclaimed, "and we are going to fight this thing!"

"You know damn well who did it!"

"Oh, yes. Now we just need to prove it!"

JT listened without interruption as his attorney told the story of two young interns from the auction house finding him on the sidewalk.

"Annabelle was dead and you were unconscious with a revolver in your hand. They took the gun, and one fetched a policeman while the other kept you covered. When the police arrived, they were told that the gun had been in your hand. Based on that, you have been named as the prime suspect. Unfortunately, they are not looking at Marcus Payne, so it will be up to us to prove he did it!" Bernstein concluded.

"How is Madeline taking this?" JT asked.

"Not well. She is not coming out of her room and is obviously very upset!"

JT stood up and walked to the cell door. "Well, we need to get me out of here!"

"Yes, I think that is possible. You are, after all, a wealthy man. You will most likely get bail because of that, but it's going to be expensive."

"I don't care about the money. I am going to nail that guy to the wall if it's the last thing I do. I know you are a criminal defense attorney, and I'm told one of the best, but if you don't want to take this project on, just tell me."

"Oh, I wouldn't miss it for the world! I didn't know Annabelle long, but I thought we might become friends."

"Well, she thought the world of you, Mr. Bernstein, so you are hired. Now get me out of here and let's get to work!"

JT stood in front of the judge of the day. Though the prosecutor was a man with little hair and no taste in clothing, it was apparent that he exuded intelligence. *He will not be a*

pushover, JT thought. On the other hand, he had one of the best criminal defense attorneys in the city and he knew who the real killer was. JT looked behind him and spotted Mrs. C, Raphael, and Michel Pierre. They waved at him and Raphael gave him a thumbs up. He nodded with a small smile.

The judge entered the courtroom, looking down at Bernstein. "Nice to see you again in my courtroom, Mort. How is your wife doing these days?"

"She is fine, your honor, and sends her greetings!" Bernstein replied with a wide grin.

"Well, tell her hello for me and don't forget to get me on the apple pie list when fall rolls around!" the judge said.

The prosecutor rolled his eyes as Bernstein nudged JT.

The judge read out the preliminaries, then looked at JT, who was standing ramrod straight in a tailored suit, freshly shaven and looking nothing like a killer. "Well, Mr. Thomas, I understand you have come into a great deal of money recently. And according to the prosecutor, you killed your fiancée in cold blood."

The prosecutor nodded while JT shook his head. "No sir, I did not kill her," he stated.

"Well, this is not the time for you to make declarations, sir," the judge replied. "The purpose of this arraignment is to decide whether to grant bail." He looked at the prosecutor. "So, Mr. Perlman, what say you about bail?"

The prosecutor stood up and declared firmly, "This is a capital offense, a murder of lovers. This person is a newcomer to our fair city and has recently become wealthy, in the state's estimation, through potentially dubious means, and we believe he is a flight risk. The state calls for no bail!"

The judge looked down. "Dubious means," he said with a smile. "Well, this trial, if there is to be one, has nothing to do with how anyone became wealthy. This man is charged with murder and I don't care how long he has been in the city. We were all new at one time, Mr. 'Came in from Philadelphia' Perlman!"

The prosecutor nodded and examined the tops of his unpolished shoes, head down.

The judge turned toward the defense attorney. "So, Mr. Bernstein, what have you to say about this 'newcomer?' Is there any reason we shouldn't keep him locked up?"

Bernstein stood up. "Well, not surprisingly, we disagree with our esteemed prosecutor. Mr. Thomas is a law-abiding citizen of Colorado. He has never, and I repeat never, been arrested or charged with anything at all in his life. He served his country well in the late war, rising to the rank of lieutenant colonel. He served as a federal marshal in Kansas, where he was credited with cleaning up the God-forsaken town of Coffeeville. He is a friend of the governor of Colorado, and from what I'm told has brought numerous bank robbers and murderers to justice. Witnesses will attest that he is generous to a fault. In my estimation, he is a fine upstanding citizen. Therefore, I submit that no bail is appropriate. He is no flight risk. He wants to clear his name and see the real perpetrator, the man who murdered the woman he loves, behind bars!"

The judge sat silent for a minute, jotting notes. He looked at the prosecutor, then at JT. "I am setting the bail at one million dollars," he declared. "Mr. Thomas is not to leave New York unless it is cleared by my office. I am freezing the rest of his assets as well. Beyond the one million, that is."

Addressing the prosecutor, he said, "I must tell you, something smells fishy about this and I'm surprised that you even brought charges, but that's what trials are for," he said, and stood up to leave.

"Court is adjourned. Don't forget about my apple pie," he said, with a smile and a wink in Bernstein's direction.

JT left the courthouse, temporarily a free man. "That went well," he said to the smiling attorney.

"Yes, it certainly did! Luck of the draw," Bernstein said with a smile. "Judge Bailey was never a prosecutor. He started as a defense lawyer and has never forgotten his roots. Not to mention he just doesn't like Mr. Perlman," he said with a chuckle.

"What's the chance that we get him in a trial if it comes to that?"

"I would think very good. This is a high-profile case and normally he should get to choose if he wants to keep it. The

New York court system likes the idea of continuity," he said with a sparkle in his eye. "I think we should petition the court for a speedy trial and waive the right to a jury. A jury may look at your newfound wealth and throw the book at you just for spite, especially if they find out about the auction and that the Rockefellers bought your Crown Jewels."

JT nodded. "Well, you're the expert. I'll trust your judgment."

Bernstein put his arm across JT's shoulders. "I believe this is going to turn out better than I hoped. I'll petition the court this afternoon and get things rolling!"

JT rode in the carriage with the group from the hotel. They were all excited about the hearing, and all agreed it was going better than expected. JT accepted their premature congratulations with a smile.

Back at the hotel, he started up the stairs to Maddy's room just as she stuck her head out of the café. She saw him and flew into his arms, giving him a sobbing hug. He looked at the gathered staff, shaking his head. They got the message and quietly left JT and Maddy, now both crying uncontrollably, at the bottom of the stairs.

Afterward, JT took his handkerchief out of his pocket and handed it to Maddy. "Let's sit in the café. I'd like to get a cup of coffee and have a talk."

Maddy wiped her eyes and nodded, then took JT's hand and led the way. "Would you like something to eat?" she asked. "We saved some lunch for you. I'll bet you're starving."

JT looked up at her as his stomach growled loudly, and Maddy actually smiled. "Well, I guess that answers my question. I'll be back in a minute," she said.

She soon returned with coffee and sat down. "Michel Pierre is making us something," she said with a smile.

"I don't know what to say or how to start," JT said quietly.

"Tell me about it," Maddy replied. "Don't leave anything out."

JT looked into her eyes and saw a remarkable resolve. "All right, let me start with the auction…"

"Then I woke up staring at the ceiling in a jail cell, accused of your mother's murder," he concluded.

"Oh my God!" Maddy exclaimed. "So how are you here?"

"We had a bail hearing today and it went well. I'm out on bail and Mr. Bernstein, my attorney, thinks we may be able to get this whole thing thrown out of court."

"That's wonderful!"

"Well, we shall see."

Maddy hung her head. "I just can't believe this is really happening. We had a wonderful trip together and really started to get close again. She told me about being captured by the Cheyenne, you rescuing her and the other gals…everything!"

JT nodded, looking off into space.

"She was so in love with you, even though you hadn't known each other for a long time. She said you had gone through so much together and she finally found the love of her life!" Maddy said, a tear escaping from her eye.

"I know. I felt the same way," JT said quietly.

It was three weeks until the trial. JT spent part of each day at Bernstein's offices, going through his testimony step by step. Meanwhile, Gregor Nelson had returned from Colorado. His investigative skills were brought to bear on JT's case. He immediately set out to discover why their carriage never arrived. He also vowed to surreptitiously check out Marcus Payne and his buddy the sheriff. JT knew he had a late start, but he was glad Gregor was back and standing in his corner. Bernstein was confident, but Gregor's attention to detail and preparation were second to none.

JT got so tired of telling and retelling his story that he finally threw his hands in the air, crying, "Enough!"

Chapter Twenty-Eight

Finally, the day of the trial arrived. Mrs. C, Raphael, and Michel Pierre accompanied JT. Madeline was not going to come. She simply didn't want to witness it and she did not want to see her father again. She was certain of what had really happened, as was the group. Marcus Payne had murdered Annabelle.

JT and Bernstein sat at the defense table. The prosecutor, nicely dressed in a pressed, off-the-rack plain gray suit, sat with his assistant. Both were smiling and chuckling. JT turned to his attorney with a frown. "What are they so happy about?" he asked.

Bernstein shook his head. "They are nervous, that's all. Pretrial jitters. I used to either laugh or throw up in my early days. Don't worry about it!"

JT glanced past the prosecutor's table just as Marcus Payne and his shadow the sheriff sat down, smiling and chuckling. Marcus looked at JT with an evil look in his eyes. He smiled deviously and slashed his finger across his throat.

JT frowned, with an anxious pit growling in his stomach. *What the hell was that all about?*

The bailiff stood and announced the judge, who came flying up the steps to his leather chair. JT heard Bernstein groan. It was not Judge Bailey, but Judge Cavanaugh. And he had a wide grin on his face.

"Well, well, well," he said, looking straight at JT. "I haven't seen you since the auction. I guess you've been a busy man! You just couldn't leave well enough alone, could you?"

He frowned at Bernstein, then nodded to the prosecutor. "My, my, what a dandy suit, Mr. Perlman. Very nice!" The prosecutor nodded and smiled.

"I understand there will be no jury at the defense's request, which suits me just fine. This shouldn't take long. It is obvious what has happened here," he said, scowling angrily at JT. "But that's what trials are for. I am going to curtail the opening statements and add a few minutes to the ending statements since this is really a cut-and-dried case."

He looked at the prosecutor. "You are up first, Mr. Perlman. Have at it!" he bellowed.

The prosecutor stood. "Your honor, we agree this should be short and sweet!"

Bernstein jumped up. "Objection, your honor!"

"Overruled. Now sit down at shut up," the judge barked. "Please continue, Mr. Perlman."

"We call Sean Cubert of Williams and Williams Auctioneers as our first witness," Perlman said.

Sean took the witness stand and was sworn in. "State your name and your occupation," Perlman said.

"My name is Sean Cubert, and I am senior auctioneer at Williams and Williams."

"Let me ask you, were people allowed to bring firearms into the building during the auction?"

"No, not at all. It is prohibited. We had six armed guards on hand, so it was also unnecessary," he stated succinctly.

"So, no one could have brought in, say, a revolver, and stuck it in a belt behind him?"

Cubert pondered the question, "Well, we certainly don't frisk our patrons, and these were the most wealthy and respectable citizens of New York. So yes, someone could have done that. But if anyone had produced a gun, they would have been cut down by our guards in a New York heartbeat," he said with a chuckle.

"Yes, I'm sure they are most formidable," Perlman replied. "However, what if the necklace were not the intended target? What if, instead, someone brought the weapon to use after the auction? For instance, with the intention of shooting his fiancée?"

Bernstein jumped up. "Conjecture, your honor!"

"Overruled," Cavanaugh snapped, "and if you don't sit down, I'm going to hold you in contempt and have you in a cell."

Bernstein sat down, shaking his head and cursing under his breath. The judge nodded at the prosecutor to continue.

"So, is that possible?" Perlman asked the witness.

"Of course," the auctioneer replied.

"I'm finished with this witness," Perlman concluded.

Bernstein stood up and walked slowly to the witness. "Nice to see you again. So, the auction went well?"

"Oh, absolutely. It was one of the finest pieces we have ever auctioned," Cubert replied.

Bernstein turned and pointed toward JT. "Do you recognize this gentleman?"

"Yes, that is JT Thomas. He was our primary client that night."

"Do you remember a briefing with Mr. Thomas and myself where you indicated that you would have six guards armed with shotguns?"

"Oh yes, of course."

"Do you remember what JT's response was?"

"Oh, yes. Actually, it was quite humorous. He said, 'Then I guess I won't need this!' Then he pulled his pistol out of his holster."

Bernstein leaned forward. "Did you say his holster?"

"Why yes, of course."

"Not from behind his back?"

"Ah, no, not from behind the back."

"How about from behind his neck?"

"Ah…no…"

"How about out of his…" Bernstein bellowed, making a motion toward his rear end.

The prosecutor leapt up. "I object!" he said, looking at the judge.

"I withdraw the question," Bernstein said. "So, if Mr. Thomas brought a gun to the auction in a holster, would you have relieved him of it?"

The auctioneer thought for a moment. "No, it was his auction, so he could bring a gun. But he knew we were going to be adequately prepared and I'm sure he saw no need."

"So, he would have had no need to conceal a weapon at the auction?"

"I would think not!"

The prosecutor quickly stood to object, but the judge waved him down and pointed at Cubert. "That is conjecture, and you have no basis in fact to be making such kinds of statements," he said.

Cubert slumped over in his seat, chastised.

"No more questions for this witness," Bernstein said with a brief chuckle as he sat down.

The next witness was Christopher Fleishman, the intern who had found JT and Annabelle in the street. Perlman moved toward the witness box. "Mr. Fleishman, I understand you are an intern at Williams and Williams auction house?"

"Yes sir," Fleischman answered.

"Do I also understand that you discovered JT Thomas and the deceased Annabelle on the sidewalk near the auction house?"

"Yes sir, that is correct. I was on my way home after the auction when I saw them."

"Excellent. Is that your normal route home?"

"Yes sir, it is."

"Good, good. Now tell the court what you found on the sidewalk," Perlman said, waving at the crowded room.

"Well, I was walking with my colleague Tiffany and we found Mr. Thomas and Miss Annabelle on the sidewalk. She seemed like she was dead because she wasn't moving and she had a bloody hole in her chest. Mr. Thomas was a little distance away from her near a brick wall. I thought he was dead as well since he was not moving. He had a gun in his hand and it seemed clear to me that he had shot Miss Annabelle."

Bernstein rose to object, but before he could utter a sound the angry judge held up a hand. "Overruled!" he growled, then nodded to the witness. "Please continue."

The prosecutor smiled at Fleischman. "How did you surmise that? You said he wasn't moving and yet you thought he killed his fiancée. How could that have happened?"

"Well, when I knelt down to take the gun out of his hand he moved, and I noticed that the back of his head was a bit bloody. It looked like he slipped after shooting her."

"Slipped? How would he have slipped?"

"Oh, it rained a bit during the auction and that sidewalk is slippery when it rains."

"So, you surmised that JT Thomas killed his fiancée after a wildly successful auction, slipped and hit his head on the edge of a brick wall and knocked himself out? Is that what you are saying?"

Bernstein started to stand up to object, but the judge swiveled and simply shook his head, so he shrugged and sat down with a scowl on his face.

Perlman turned to the judge. "I have no more questions for this witness, but I want to congratulate him on his wisdom and his perception. He clearly understands what he saw on the night of the auction," he stated with a broad grin.

Bernstein stood up and looked at the smiling witness. JT looked at his counsel and shook his head. "No questions for this witness at this time," Bernstein said quietly.

Judge Cavanaugh banged his gavel. Looking at the clock, he said, "It's a bit early, but let's break for lunch. Please return at one o'clock, promptly."

Chapter Twenty-Nine

As they left the courtroom, all of the folks from the hotel converged on JT, asking what had happened to the good judge, and who was the bad judge.

Bernstein stepped in front of JT. "We are as surprised as you are, but we need to regroup, so please excuse us." He took JT by the arm, gesturing at Gregor Nelson to join them.

JT looked angrily at his attorney. "This is not going well at all. Cavanaugh seems like he is ready to hang me in the courtroom. We need to do something or I'm going to get convicted of murder!"

Bernstein simply nodded with a scowl on his beet-red face.

They found an unoccupied conference room. JT slammed the door and turned to his shrunken defense attorney. "I thought you said that the judge who presides at the bail hearing is normally assigned the case!" he shouted.

"Yes, I did, and that's normally the way it works, but, but, I just don't know what happened," Bernstein replied, hanging his head.

Gregor Nelson leaned forward and cleared his throat. "Oh, I know exactly what happened," he said.

JT looked across the table. "Well, please tell us. At this rate, they are going to convict me of murder before suppertime!"

Gregor sat back. "Here is what happened. Mr. Bernstein, I don't suppose your wife has made any apple pies lately?"

"No, not for another week."

"I was certain of that. Well, someone delivered a pie to Judge Baily two days ago, claiming it was from your wife. The next day, he was stricken with a severe case of food poisoning! According to his doctor, he's out of action for at least a week."

JT stared straight ahead, shaking his head in disbelief.

"But I have some good news! I found your carriage driver. He was approached by a man flashing a badge. He said he had talked to you, JT, and that you were going to be riding in Mr. Bernstein's carriage. Then he told the driver to take him to the Fifth Avenue Tavern. He was instructed to wait for an hour, and if the man didn't come out, he was to head back to the stable. Which is what happened."

JT stood up abruptly. "Why would the driver do that?"

"Simple. He was tipped fifty dollars."

Bernstein looked up. "This is good news. We need to get this driver on the witness stand, as well as the sheriff. But we need to surreptitious about it. These men are killers and I don't want to be responsible for the death of the carriage driver!"

Gregor looked at his watch. "You best be getting back. I'm going to find that driver again. I told him what's going on and he feels terrible about Annabelle. As long as he's around, I'm sure I can get him here immediately."

"That's wonderful," Bernstein replied. "I'll call the sheriff to the stand and you bring the driver in afterward!"

JT and Bernstein returned just as Cavanaugh came out of his chambers. "Well, I hope everyone had a nice lunch," he said to the crowded courtroom. "Mr. Perlman, please continue."

The prosecutor stood up. "Your honor, we rest our case." He paused. "Unless Mr. Thomas would like to testify?" he said with a laugh.

The judge replied, "Well, we can't compel him to. That is up to the accused and his counsel, as you well know."

The prosecutor nodded and sat down.

Bernstein stood up quickly. "The defense calls Sheriff Xavier Duvall to the stand!" he bellowed.

The sheriff was taken by surprise but made his way slowly to the witness stand. He was sworn in and turned with a sneer to the defense attorney.

Bernstein leaned forward. "So, Sheriff, how are you today?"

"What do you care?" Duvall responded.

Bernstein laughed. "Just being polite, Sheriff, just being polite, but if you want to skip the pleasantries that is most certainly OK with me!" He moved into Duvall's space, sniffing deeply. "So, I trust you had a good lunch?"

"I thought you said we were going to skip the pleasantries, as you put it? Besides, it's none of your business!" Duvall yelled.

"I am, Sheriff, I am. I just wanted to know if you make a habit of consuming alcohol at lunch."

Duvall sat back. "Not usually, but Marcus and I decided to celebrate. You are going to lose this case and everyone knows it!" he declared, looking at Marcus Payne with a smirk.

Bernstein smiled. "We will get to Marcus Payne soon enough, but for now I'd like to talk about you. By the way, are you formally on duty today?"

"Well, yeah, sure, but there is no law against having a drink at lunch," Duvall replied in a strained voice.

Bernstein stepped back and looked at the judge. "Well, your department's regulations must be different from the New York police department's. Here in this great city we don't allow our officers to imbibe while they are on duty, celebration or not!" he bellowed as the judge nodded and frowned.

"But be that as it may, answer me this," Bernstein continued. "Were you at the auction at Williams and Williams on August 24th?

"Well, sure. What a dumb question; you saw me there," Duvall replied with a scowl.

"Oh yes, of course I did, didn't I? Weren't you sitting with your pal Marcus Payne?"

Duvall nodded. "Speak up, Sheriff, please speak up," Bernstein said.

"Yes, I was with him. I sat right next to him, as you well know. What's that got to do with anything?"

Bernstein glanced at the judge. "Do you have courtrooms in your county, Sheriff?"

"Well, of course we do."

"Excellent. And in those courtrooms, does the witness ask the questions or does the attorney ask the questions?"

Duvall looked down. "Ah, the damn lawyer," he said.

Bernstein laughed loudly. "Damn lawyer! That's the first thing you have said that makes any sense! Anyway, let's get back to the auction. Where did you enter the auction house? Was it the back door, the side door, or the front doors?"

"Why are you asking these damn dumb questions? I went in and out the front doors like everyone in the auditorium. I don't need to be sneaking in a side entrance like a servant or a damn delivery man!"

"No, indeed you don't. I would imagine you pretty much go in and out any entrance you want, being a sheriff and all."

"You bet I do."

"So, you saw all the carriages line up out front, did you not?"

Duvall looked up at the judge. "Why is he asking me these stupid questions?"

The judge scowled at him. "Just answer the damn question!"

Duvall looked at the floor, realizing where this was going. "Yes, I saw them," he whispered.

"Good, good. Boy, there sure were a lot of them, and fancy as well! So, did you come in a carriage, Sheriff?"

Duvall looked up with fear on his face. "No sir, I did not," he replied softly.

"And Sheriff, did you leave in a carriage?" Bernstein bellowed.

Just then, the courtroom door opened. The carriage driver and Gregor Nelson sat down in the gallery, in plain view of the judge and the sheriff.

Duvall slumped down and nodded slightly. "Yes, I did. I left with him," he said, pointing to the driver.

"Ah. Any idea whose carriage you were taking?" Bernstein asked as Duvall tried to disappear into the chair. "Did you hear me, Sheriff?"

Duvall exhaled loudly and sat up slowly until he was erect in the witness chair. He turned away from the carriage driver, who had a look of scorn on his face. "You know the answer to that," he said, pointing at JT. "It was his."

Bernstein turned toward the judge. "No further questions, your honor."

The judge looked at the shocked prosecutor. "Your witness," he said.

"No questions for this witness at this time," the prosecutor said forlornly.

Bernstein stood up. "Then the defense calls Antony Bianchi to the stand," he bellowed.

Bianchi took the stand with a look of satisfaction and was sworn in.

"Mr. Bianchi, are you a carriage driver for Langford Stables?" Bernstein asked.

"Yes, sir, I am," Bianchi replied proudly.

"Sheriff Duvall has told this court that you gave him a ride away from the Williams and Williams auction on August 24th. Is that correct?"

Bianchi blushed, but replied in a clear voice, "Yes, sir, it is."

"Now, why would you have done that? The carriage was leased to Annabelle Hewitt and JT Thomas, was it not?"

"Yes, but the sheriff climbed into the cab and showed me his badge. He said JT and Annabelle had another ride. He then told me to pull out of the lineup and take him to the Fifth Avenue Tavern."

"And did you do so?"

"Yes, I did."

"And what did you do when you got there?"

"I parked the carriage and he went in to the tavern. It was very crowded."

"So then you left and came back to pick up your original fare?"

"Ah, no. The sheriff told me to wait an hour. If he didn't come out, I was to go straight back to the stable."

"And did you?"

"Yes, I did."

"And what compelled you to do this? After all, you only had a stranger's word on this arrangement!"

Bianchi hung his head. "The sheriff, he gave me fifty dollars and told me I should keep this to myself."

"Ah," replied Bernstein. "One more question. Do you read the Bible?"

"Yes, I do, every morning!"

"So you know who Judas Iscariot is, don't you?" he asked quietly. "Annabelle Hewitt, whom you drove for a month, is dead, and it was a direct result of your actions that she was murdered in cold blood! All for fifty pieces of silver!"

As Bianchi wept quietly on the stand, Bernstein turned toward the gallery. "But although the sheriff set the trap, he didn't pull the trigger. Nor, obviously, did Mr. Thomas. No, the murderer is sitting in this very courtroom!" he bellowed, pointing at the obviously inebriated Marcus Payne.

Everyone in the courtroom looked at Marcus, and the prosecutor leaped up. "Objection!" he yelled.

The judge immediately responded. "Sustained!" he said, glowering at Bernstein.

"I withdraw the pointed finger," Bernstein said. "No more questions for this witness."

Judge Cavanaugh looked down at the prosecutor, who simply shook his head.

"It is late, and after that display, I think we should call it a day," he said. "Mr. Payne, I'm guessing Mr. Bernstein is going to call you tomorrow as a witness. I expect you to be here at 9 a.m. sharp."

He stood up, looked over the courtroom, and banged his gavel. "Court dismissed, and we will reconvene tomorrow morning at nine!"

Chapter Thirty

Nine o'clock arrived and Cavanaugh emerged from his chambers. JT and Bernstein rose, as did everyone in the courtroom. Maddy was seated behind JT with the rest of the hotel contingent.

The judge nodded to both attorneys. "Good morning to everyone," he said, looking around the courtroom. "So where is Mr. Payne?"

Bernstein replied, "We haven't seen him," just as the courtroom doors opened and a disheveled Marcus Payne entered. He was wearing the same suit as yesterday and reeked of booze, so much so that the people that he sat next to rose quickly and moved away.

Cavanaugh shook his head and nodded to Bernstein. "It's your show."

The bailiff called Marcus to the witness chair. After he was sworn in, Bernstein approached him. "Good morning, Mr. Payne. And how are you on this fine sunny morning?" he bellowed.

Marcus looked up. "Good morning, my ass. I hate morning and I don't give a damn about sunshine!" he replied.

Bernstein looked at the judge, who was chuckling softly and shaking his head. "Well, I guess you're a night owl," Bernstein said, as he sniffed the air around the witness.

"Are you going to ask me a question, or should I just go home to bed?" Marcus snapped.

"Oh, I have a question. Did you know that Annabelle Hewitt was planning on divorcing you?"

"Well, hell yes, everyone knew that and your lackey served me with the damn papers!"

The judge banged his gavel. "Enough of this swearing. I should have stopped it yesterday, there are ladies present," he said, nodding to the gallery. "I'm the only one who gets to swear in my courtroom," he said with a grin.

Bernstein smiled and resumed his questioning, "OK, so you knew the divorce was imminent, but since your wife was brutally murdered before you got divorced, I guess you inherit all her worldly possessions! Don't you?"

Marcus leaned forward. "Yeah, I guess I do."

"So now you have all the money you will ever need!"

"I was rich before, thanks to my mother, God rest her soul."

"Really? Did you know your wife was worth well over six million dollars when she died?"

"Well yeah, I mean I was there at the auction. But I loved Annabelle and I didn't want a divorce!" Marcus said quietly.

"Yes, but you knew you couldn't prevent it and you saw an opportunity to become a multimillionaire. And so you killed her, didn't you!" Bernstein bellowed.

Marcus sat up and began to sob. "No, I didn't. I loved her."

Bernstein walked over to the bailiff and asked him for the murder weapon. He turned so Marcus and the courtroom could see it. "Do you recognize this Colt revolver?" he asked, handing it to Marcus.

Marcus quickly set it on the wide railing as if it were poison. "I've never seen it before!" he said loudly.

Madeline leaned forward, obviously shaken, and whispered in JT's ear. "Are you sure?" asked JT, loud enough for the judge to hear.

Cavanaugh looked over. "Excuse me; we are trying to conduct a trial here!"

"I'm sorry, your honor, but the court needs to hear this!" JT replied. "This is Madeline, Mr. Payne's daughter."

Cavanaugh nodded at Maddy. "Yes, and what of it?"

"Well, perhaps she should explain."

The prosecutor jumped up. "I object, your honor. The witness is out of order."

The judge looked over at him. "I imagine you would object, and I don't blame you."

He motioned for Maddy to come up next to the bench. "Whisper to me," he said.

He listened for a bit, then his eyes got as big as saucers. "Repeat that!" he said. Maddy bent down and whispered again.

Cavanaugh reached out and held Madeline's elbow, turning her toward the courtroom. He looked down at the anxious prosecutor. "Overruled," he said. "I'm going to depart from normal procedure. Mr. Thomas is right; the court needs to hear what Mr. Payne's daughter has to say."

After she was summarily sworn in, he turned to Madeline and nodded. "Go ahead."

Maddy stood straight and looked out at the courtroom. "As the judge said, I am Madeline Payne, daughter to Marcus Payne and Annabelle Hewitt." She paused, wiping a tear away at the mention of her mother. "That gun is certainly familiar to me, and I know it is familiar to my father," she said, looking at him with a frown on her face. "That's because I gave that gun to him three years ago for his birthday!"

The prosecutor jumped up. "I object! That is a common Colt revolver! There are thousands of them made every year!" he said, looking hopefully at the judge.

Cavanaugh shook his head. "Overruled," he said. He turned to Madeline. "Go on, continue."

"As I said, I gave my father that gun. I recognized it from the ebony grip. And if you'll look at the bottom of the frame, you'll see where I had his name engraved."

Cavanaugh looked at Marcus, who was panting and turning red in the face. "Go ahead, Mr. Payne, turn it over and read what is engraved there," he ordered.

Marcus gingerly grabbed the Colt and turned it over, staring at the engraving. He looked at Madeline. "Why, why?" he said in a whisper. "I'm your father!"

"And she was my mother! You killed her, you drunken animal!" Maddy screamed.

Marcus grabbed the revolver by the barrel and threw it at Maddy, nearly hitting her in the face. He vaulted over the railing and stumbled after her as she shrieked and ran for the doors. The judge and the attorneys froze, as did the courtroom. Just as Marcus reached the last row, a gray-haired lady stuck her cane out across his ankles, tripping him and causing him to thud into the doors.

The bailiff turned Marcus over and snapped handcuffs onto the stunned witness, then dragged him back to the front of the court and stood him in front of the judge.

Bernstein handed the Colt to the judge, who looked at the engraving. "Marcus Payne," he read aloud to the courtroom. Marcus stood defeated, hanging his head.

"Marcus Payne, I'm ordering the bailiff to arrest you for the murder of your wife Annabelle Hewitt!" Cavanaugh proclaimed. He turned to the prosecutor. "Anything to add, Mr. Perlman?"

"Ahem, the state withdraws the charges against Mr. John Thurgood Thomas," Perlman said quietly.

Cavanaugh looked at a beaming JT. "You are free to go, Mr. Thomas, and please accept the court's condolences for your loss." He stood up and banged his gavel.

"Court is dismissed, and have a nice sunny day!" he said with a smile.

Epilogue

IT stood alone at Annabelle's grave, a dozen red roses in his hand. A morning fog softened the light and a cat watched from a distance. He took off his hat.

"I am sorry I missed your funeral, but I hope you understand," he said quietly. I am not very good at those kinds of things, and I honestly don't know how I would have held up. If only I'd…"

He shook his head, then knelt and placed the flowers on the fresh mound. "Maybe it's my way of not letting you go. And it must be working, because I still feel like you're here, like I could just turn around and see your smile."

He let out a long sigh. "Anyway, here's what's going on. Gregor Nelson and I are heading back to Colorado to secure the cave and whatever else might be in it. Gregor is anxious to return. I think he's sweet on Emma," he said, smiling weakly.

"Maddy has a suite at her new hotel. Yes, I signed it over to her. She's promised to visit me in Colorado soon. Timothy took a job as the night manager. That boy sure does dote on your girl, and I can't imagine a better protector. And guess what? Mrs. C and Raphael are getting married. Lucky them, huh? Oh, you know what she called me? A good egg. I had to turn around quick when she said that."

JT's faced turned grim. "Marcus is still in jail, waiting on his sentence. I wish they'd ask me; I'd just empty my Colt into him. And Sheriff Duvall is on the run with a bounty on him as an accessory to your murder."

He rose and put his hat on. "I just wanted to see you before I go. We're all getting together tonight for dinner at the Waldorf to celebrate my acquittal. I don't feel much like celebrating, but..."

He started to leave, then stopped and turned around. "Oh yeah, one strange thing. When we were gathering your things, no one could find that necklace with the golden sleigh bells. Maybe you hid it somewhere?"

JT stood quietly with his hand on the headstone, then turned and briefly caught a glimpse of red in the forest. The red flashed, seeming to move from tree to tree. As JT strained to catch another look, it flashed again. It seemed to be red fur. "Annabelle? Annabelle?" he whispered.

He stood silently for a moment and could have sworn he heard sleigh bells, golden sleigh bells.

And he smiled.

Acknowledgements

I'd like to acknowledge the contributions to this book. I simply could not have done it without the encouragement and support of Michael Cooley, Patrick Cooley, Tom Derrick, Ann Fleischauer, and Mark Fleischauer. Thanks also to my editors and friends Ken Schubert and Melinda Nelson as well as cover designer Ivan Cakić.

Finally, I wrote this, my first novel, with the encouragement, help and support of my wonderful wife Paula. As a nurse and a horse person, she gave me timely and wise advice. Her final editing of the book was very much appreciated and thorough. It was her idea to name the horses Pete and Re-Pete, and I smile every time I think about their names.

Thank you all. I'm very grateful.

About the Author

E. Alan Fleischauer is a certified financial planner, an active member of numerous non-profit organizations, and a rock 'n' roll drummer. He lives just west of the Mississippi River, an easy ride to his Wisconsin cabin.

COMING SOON

From Hunted, book two in the JT Thomas saga.

In JT's experience, a Wanted poster called for "Dead or Alive" or simply "Alive." But just "Dead"? Now that was a new one to him. As he gazed at the image of his own weather-beaten face on the faded paper, he understood that someone wanted him gone.

A shiver ran like lightning from his sun-burnt scalp to the dust-covered toes of his boots, and he knew.

Marcus Payne.